Jake's arm slid around her waist

"These tight-fitting jodhpurs look sensational on you." The touch of his hand lightly traced her hips.

Tamsin tried to slip out of range but his fingers rippled up her spine until they reached her neck. Gently he brought her face closer to his own, his lips hovering above hers.

It was her chance to draw back, but while she wavered, he lowered his head until his lips rested lightly on hers. Then the kiss deepened, gradually bringing with it a fiery confusion of emotion that left Tamsin breathless.

She stepped hastily back. "You shouldn't do that to complete strangers," she croaked.

"We're not strangers." Jake spoke softly, reaching out to touch her hair. "We're not strangers, Tamsin, not us."

Sally Heywood is a British author, born in Yorkshire. After leaving university, she had several jobs, including running an art gallery, a guest house and a boutique. She has written several plays for the theater and television, in addition to her romance novels for Harlequin. Her special interests are sailing, reading, fashion, interior decorating and helping in a children's nursery.

Books by Sally Heywood

HARLEQUIN ROMANCE
2925—IMPOSSIBLE TO FORGET

HARLEQUIN PRESENTS
1200—FANTASY LOVER
1235—TODAY, TOMORROW, AND FOREVER
1256—LAW OF LOVE

TRUST ME, MY LOVE

Sally Heywood

Harlequin Books

TORONTO • NEW YORK • LONDON
AMSTERDAM • PARIS • SYDNEY • HAMBURG
STOCKHOLM • ATHENS • TOKYO • MILAN

Original hardcover edition published in 1989
by Mills & Boon Limited

ISBN 0-373-03074-6

Harlequin Romance first edition September 1990

This Book Is Dedicated to
Lucie Sonderer
With Love and Gratitude

CHAPTER ONE

A SEA breeze tousled Tamsin's red-gold curls as she leaned on the rail of the ship and watched the coast of France recede into the hazy distance. There was a little sinking feeling in the pit of her stomach as she realised what she had done. When she let Emile talk her into returning to England, all she could think was that she was saving her father's good name. It took some time before all the ramifications hit her.

Now she gave an involuntary shudder. Regrets were already beginning to crowd in thick and fast, but it was too late for second thoughts. She was on her way.

Glancing down at her watch, she guessed she would be at Rose Mead by evening. With no one to meet her she would make her way quickly through Customs and on to the boat-train to Victoria. From there it was only a short distance to the Berkshire home of Saul O'Neill, an old racing colleague of her father's, in whose house she would be staying over the next few weeks.

Saul looked after half a dozen horses for a Colonel Newman now he was retired from active racing, his farm, Rose Mead, being part of the Newmans' Brantingham Park estate. Tamsin would be having what Emile called 'a training break'— the real purpose for her stay being somewhat different.

She hated herself for the minor deception involved, but she resolved to work hard for Saul to salve her conscience, and after all, she told herself, she wasn't actually planning to harm anyone. She was glad in a way that it was Saul she was staying with, rather than a complete stranger. He had been one of her father's closest companions in the good days of sweet memory now gone forever, though since his retirement she had seen little of him. Somehow he would make the past seem less distant, the future less grim. For two pins she would stay and work for Saul for good. But first she had something to do.

She shuddered again, pulling up the collar of her new navy wool jacket, beginning to make her way across the lurching deck to the saloon where she eventually managed to find a seat, then she settled down to count the minutes until the white cliffs of home came at last into view.

Saul welcomed Tamsin with open arms. He was standing on the steps of his sandstone farmhouse, a stocky sixty-year-old, shrewd blue eyes noting her pale face even as he gave her a quick welcoming hug. A champion jockey in his day, he had ridden many of her father's horses to victory, and his cosy farmhouse kitchen was crammed with mementoes from the past. When he led her inside, one of the first things she noticed was her father's bright racing silks hanging over the mantelpiece.

'Great days, Saul,' she murmured, fingering them sadly.

'I remember you on race days, Tammy, love,' he told her as soon as they settled before the fire with cups of tea after she had taken her bags upstairs. 'Your dad used to have you dressed up like a little doll. You were the poppet of the Royal Enclosure, all curls and smiles!'

'Those were the days, all right!' She gazed wistfully into the crackling flames of the log fire. 'I expect I was a bit of a brat in those days. Dad used to spoil me rotten, didn't he?'

Saul shook his head. 'You were a little cracker. He had great hopes for you as a show-jumper.'

She caught his eye and gave a rueful grimace. 'If he were alive now he'd be pretty disappointed to discover that I've given it up.'

'If he were alive now, you wouldn't have had to give it up,' replied Saul. He leaned over and patted her hand. 'Don't feel down, pet. You've only missed one season. You'll find somebody willing to let you ride for them before long.'

'But it won't be the same as having my own horses, Saul. It'll never be the same.' She tried to shrug it off. 'It was so good when Dad was——' Her voice dropped. 'Before the accident, that is.' She tried to give him one of her old smiles, but her green eyes were already misting over. She leaned forward, letting a veil of sherry-gold hair conceal her expression. 'Do you remember that pony I had when I was ten?' she asked brightly, trying to change the subject.

Saul gave a chuckle. 'Topper, you mean? Little devils, the pair of you!'

'Every time we appeared smothered in rosettes, a groan must have gone up!' She gave a shaky laugh.

'You were a brilliant little rider even then,' he told her. 'It's a crying shame the horses had to be sold off. You were all set to make a real name for yourself.'

Tamsin avoided his glance, wishing he hadn't gone back to the same theme. She had made a real effort over the last season not to think about her suddenly ended career, and how instead she had got a lowly job as groom at a racing stables across the Channel, resolutely refusing even to follow the news of who was in and who was out in the fast-changing world of show-jumping because it was too painful not to be part of it any longer. She'd cut it right out, as if it had never been the centre of her life.

Saul patted her hand again. 'You could get back your old form if you gave it a try...'

'I expect I could,' she agreed, unable to disguise her heartache for a moment, 'but without sound financial backing we both know it's impossible to start up again. It's not a game for amateurs.'

Saul looked thoughtfully into the fire then. He seemed to be weighing something in his mind, his gnarled old face heavy with thought. When he looked up again, there was a light of challenge in his eyes that Tamsin recognised at once, and even though his words were casual she knew him well enough to realise there was some deeper purpose behind what he said. 'You ought to think hard about this job of yours with Emile de Monterrey,' he admonished unexpectedly. 'You've been away from home too long. And it's not doing your career any good working for an outfit like that.'

She gave a short laugh. 'He's my bread and butter now, Saul. That is my career.'

Saul gave an exclamation and his glance swept the fine features of the girl sitting opposite with a look of compassion. As a child she had been the apple of her father's eye, and he guessed she hadn't found it easy since he'd died, leaving her without a penny to her name. He could imagine what a struggle it had been, and how it was pride now that made her say her career as a show-jumper was over. He took out his pipe. 'Get yourself nicely settled in here first. Then give it a bit of thought.' He puffed a couple of times to light the tobacco in his pipe, then added in his slow country burr, 'I can understand why you wanted to get out straight after the funeral, what with all that hullabaloo in the Press. But you ought to put that behind you and come back where you belong.'

Sadly Tamsin contemplated the blazing fire. If only she could unburden herself to Saul, she was thinking. But she dared not tell him what Emile had threatened. Saul would be one to go straight to the police, and then the whole scandal of her father's affairs would be front page news in France as well as England. It was best this way, best to keep quiet, best to try to handle it herself.

'I'll think about coming back,' she told him. 'It would be lovely. I've missed you.'

'Jake'll be over the moon to find Teddy Harland's daughter living next door,' Saul went on, puffing contentedly now his pipe was alight.

'Jake? Jake Newman?' Tamsin gave a start. Emile and his plan came crashing painfully back into the forefront of her mind. She felt her muscles tense.

But Saul was busy with his pipe and didn't notice the change in her expression. 'He needs somebody to ride his second string for him, despite what he thinks himself. He's got too much to handle right now. Somebody with your experience is just what he needs.'

'I couldn't leave my job in France yet,' she told him, feeling ashamed and wishing for the thousandth time that she hadn't got involved; but Saul, taking his time over his pipe, settled back, a smile on his face.

'Wait till you see him. He's magic on a horse, that one,' he told her proudly. 'He'll be tipped to make the British team this summer, you mark my words!'

'He's magic off a horse too, judging by the Press photos!' joked Tamsin, trying to inject a little lightness into her voice. She had searched the riding magazines for references to Jake Newman and his horse Golden Boy as soon as she'd got off the train. There were plenty. He was news. His good fortune gave her an uncharacteristic twinge of jealousy. Briefly she thought, why him and not me? Then she went on to acknowledge that he deserved his success. He must have worked hard to come up from practically nowhere in the last season or so, sweeping the board at all the major competitions. Saul obviously thought highly of him. In different circumstances she would have been really pleased to be part of the Brantingham team. Now she felt like a fraud even before she'd met him.

Tamsin got her chance to come face to face with him sooner than expected.

As far as she knew he was still in the States, and he was far from her thoughts when she turned up at the stables a few days later. Although she had been taken on by Saul to help him with the half-dozen horses he was bringing on for Jake, she found she was spending as much time over at Brantingham as at Rose Mead. When one of the lads delegated to muck out was off with a cold, it seemed natural to offer to help out. It was the fourth day she had been in at crack of dawn, and she was half-way through the chores when the phrase Saul had used came slamming back to her.

Magic? Magic on a horse, maybe, she thought. Or in a Press photograph, no doubt. But standing six foot two on the cobblestones of the yard at six-thirty on a raw February morning with the rain pounding down and a ferocious scowl on his handsome features, he was anything but. She recognised him at once.

'Jet-lagged,' she muttered, not caring whether he heard or not. She hadn't expected him back yet. It was bad luck for Emile's plan that she looked so awful.

With a checked cap tipped low against the rain, the collar of her bottle-green Barbour pulled right up against the weather, and a scruffy pair of jeans and green Hunter wellies completing the picture, she might have forgiven Jake Newman for what he had just called her. But then it came again.

'Jump to it, lad!'

Lad?

When she fixed an astonished glance on him, he made matters worse by adding, 'What in hell do you call this?'

The 'this' was a loose-box that hadn't been mucked out. That it should have been by this time in the morning, Tamsin would have readily admitted, given the chance. She might even have explained the reason for this lapse from total efficiency—but for that peremptory, 'Lad! Here, lad!'

She glowered back at him, fury momentarily making her forget her purpose.

'New, are you?' He peered down at her through the gloom and the glancing rain, while she glared back at him before turning wordlessly on her heel with the intention of getting on with her job before she said something she regretted.

'Just hold on, will you?' barked the voice behind her. 'I asked you a question.'

Anger rose like a rapid scarlet tide up her body. She would never get used to being ordered about. And this was the man Emile had said she must wrap around her little finger, too!

'Who are you?' His tone was curious. 'I didn't know we'd taken on any new hands.'

'I'm working with Saul O'Neill, actually——' She hadn't meant it to sound like a plea for special concessions, but her antagonist took it as such. She saw his face cloud over.

'I don't damn well care if you're working with the Empress of Siam. Get this loose-box turned out, will you? And quick!'

'Empress? Better not let Saul hear you call him that!' she shot back. Then the ludicrousness of the image his remark conjured up made her begin to giggle.

'Wait a minute!' A puzzled frown crossed his face. Before she could stop him a hand shot out, gripping her by the shoulder, and with the other the cap was swept from off her head, letting a mass of red-gold curls come tumbling down to her shoulders.

'A girl?' Jake Newman stood stunned, and at any other time Tamsin would have laughed at the expression on his face and the way he went on fingering her cap as if it was a red-hot coal. But instead, something about being discovered like this made her draw herself up.

'May I?' She held out her hand. He looked at it as if he had never seen one before. 'My cap? Do you mind?' she insisted. The wind scudded a gust of rain into her face, and she could feel her hair lashing uncomfortably against her flushed cheeks.

Something had at last dawned in Jake Newman's mind. 'Saul O'Neill?' he muttered. 'You're actually working with Saul?'

'He used to ride for my father, Teddy Harland,' she contributed in explanation.

Jake began to laugh softly. It was an attractive sound. Tamsin watched, fascinated, as the full lips curved back over even white teeth. But his words made her spine stiffen. 'So that's who you are,' he mocked. 'Teddy Harland's debby daughter!' He gave her a searching look, then drew his lips back in a politely mocking smile once more. 'And I thought you were still twelve!' Wicked dark eyes roamed her body for a moment, then he checked himself, saying, 'So this explains the chaos he.e. Seems I'm not back a moment too soon.' He turned to go, only pausing to throw back over his shoulder, 'Old Saul trying to save Dad a bob or two by bringing in casual labour, is he?'

Tamsin was stung into action. This wasn't the effect she'd hoped to have. She hurried after him.

'Somebody was taken sick at short notice. And I offered to help out. I'm having a training break from my job at the Count de Monterrey's stables in Chantilly.' Then, as he swung round, some evil genie made her cast a slow, appraising glance over the small, though neat and well-appointed yard before gazing smoothly back into his eyes and adding, 'Mucking out a few circus horses like these presents no problems. But if a bob or two has to be saved, I don't mind helping out.'

With a deprecating smile, she jammed her cap back on her head, without bothering to push her already sopping hair back inside, turned on her heel, and marched back into the stall.

'Hold on——' he called after her. But she pretended not to hear.

'Damn him, the arrogant devil!' she seethed to one of the horses as she pushed his flanks out of the way so she could pitch-fork the used straw under his feet. Being mistaken for a lad rankled in a way it shouldn't have. The fact that Jake Newman was everything the Press cracked him up to be added to her sense of injury. But she shouldn't have let him get through to her. It was a stupid thing to do. Now she had made her task ten times more difficult.

It had all started when Emile had sent for her when she'd been living with a group of other girls in quarters above the stables at his racing complex near Chantilly, and put something to her which at the time seemed simple and straightforward.

She had been working for him for about six months and seen him only in the distance, a powerful and slightly sinister figure, the remote head of an expensive international racing operation. She had been pleased to be ignored. After the shock of her father's sudden death and the additional, different sort of shock when she discovered that all he had left behind after a flamboyant career as racehorse owner was a pile of debts, she had only wanted to crawl away out of the limelight to lick her wounds. It was bad enough to lose the only person she had ever cared for, but wounding too to find the way of life she had been used to a thing of the past. Gone were the expensive horses, the beautiful house in the country, the luxury, the travel. Now all she possessed were a few clothes and a succession of happy memories. She went through an agonising period of readjustment, and by the time she was beginning to feel strong enough to look for a way out of it Emile had noticed her, and the summons had come.

'You are out of place here, *ma belle*,' Emile had bluntly told her, eyeing her expression closely from the far side of the imposing dark wood desk when she'd entered his office.

It was evident from what he said as he outlined his suggestion that he was impressed by who she was. Teddy Harland had been a name to be reckoned with. It was only because Emile—Count Emile de Monterrey, to give him his full title—rarely stooped to enquire too closely into the backgrounds of the stable-hands that she had escaped his notice for so long. 'You are wasted here. You can be more useful to me in other ways,' he told her. 'As I, I am sure,' he smiled thinly, 'can be useful to you.'

She held her breath. Emile's black eyes lazed over her expectant face, pale in its aura of red-gold hair, and for a moment he seemed to be distracted by another thought. Then, still smiling, he started to talk of England.

'Home,' he murmured. 'I know you must miss it.'

'Yes—yes, I do,' she admitted, wondering if all he was leading up to was to give her the sack.

'Perhaps you would even like to return for a little while?' he went on, still watching her expression.

She nodded, dropping her glance. It would probably sound disloyal, but she couldn't pretend she didn't want to go back.

'Then, my dear, you shall return.'

'But how?' she had asked, widening her eyes.

'I have a little task for you. A simple task. But it requires someone like you to perform it.'

Then he had told her about Jake Newman. How he had a horse, Golden Boy, which had taken Emile's fancy. How he wanted Golden Boy, but Newman, unreasonably, had refused to negotiate. Emile scowled slightly. Then, placing his fingertips together, he gave Tamsin a careful smile. 'You, my dear, must go over to Newman and persuade him to sell.'

'But what if he refuses?'

'My dear, let me put it this way. You have considerable charm and beauty. Newman is a man susceptible to the blandishments of young women, judging by the frequency with which his photograph appears in the Press with one or another of them on his arm——'

'But——' She broke off. It seemed a deceptively simple task. There was no need to feel uneasy. At least, she couldn't put her finger on any good reason. She raised her glance. Emile was still watching her.

'You want to know what's in it for you?' he asked, misinterpreting her hesitation. 'I'll tell you. Ten per cent commission on completion of the sale.'

Tamsin blinked.

'I don't have to remind you what that will mean in terms of hard cash...'

Tamsin was silent. The money, a lot though it was, meant nothing. What was attractive was the chance to go back home to England. Perhaps once she was back she would be able to find a job with an English stable. Now the scandal of her father's financial state was old news, perhaps she dared hold her head up once more.

'I'm sorry.' She paused, still thinking it over. 'But if he doesn't want to sell, why should I try to persuade him he should?'

'Let me suggest a reason, my dear.' Despite the smoothness of his tone, there was a sudden chill in the air. The threat was unmistakable. 'You perhaps intend to muck out horses in France for the rest of your days?' He raised a thin eyebrow.

'If need be.'

'Very brave. Of course, you have a job now,' he went on smoothly. 'But it may not necessarily always be the case...' He paused significantly. 'Nor, after you leave here, will you necessarily find it easy to obtain employment elsewhere in France.' His thin lips drew back in a brief, cold smile.

'Well, I won't do it. So that's that!' She felt angry that he should think she could be so easily threatened into doing as he wanted. She drew herself up and was just about to march out of the door when he put up a hand to detain her. Then, still smiling, he began to outline details of a betting fraud that made Tamsin gape. When he told her that her own father had been involved, she could only stare in disbelief. 'No! It's a lie,' she exclaimed. 'Dad would never do a thing like that!'

To her surprise, Emile began to laugh. 'Possibly you're right, *ma belle*; stranger things have been known. But who, outside these four walls, is to know that? I can produce letters which will incriminate him beyond all doubt.'

'Letters? Then they must be forgeries!' she bit back.

'Again, *ma belle*, who is to know that until the courts decide?'

'But——' She felt confused. Was it possible for the whole sorry business of her father's financial affairs to be raked up again? Evidently it was. Emile seemed full of confidence.

'What you're saying is—if I don't persuade Jake Newman to let you buy this beastly horse, you'll drag Dad's name through the mud?'

Emile smiled and shrugged his narrow shoulders. 'You have a rather simple way of putting things, my dear. But I think you get the picture.'

'He would never have done anything dishonest. I know he wouldn't,' she repeated helplessly.

Then she began to tremble. She had never encountered anyone as cool as Emile. While she was still taking in what he had said, he came swiftly round the side of the desk and took her by the arm.

'My dear sweet child, don't look so distraught. You must know I would do nothing to make life difficult for you. All you have to do is spend a few weeks at Newman's stables and, when he's in the right mood, pop the question. If he says no, so be it.'

'But all the rest of the things you said...' she gulped.

Emile closed her eyes. 'I was simply trying to point out difficulties. I know people who would be only too glad to stir up trouble if they got their hands on the evidence. But of course, I can stop them, if I choose.'

'But what you said about Dad—I know it can't be true——'

'Everyone does things they regret, you know.'

'But Dad wouldn't do a thing like that.'

'Unfortunately, not everyone will believe you.'

Bitterly Tamsin remembered the scandal in the Press when her father's financial state had become public knowledge. There were always people around ready to point the finger. Humiliated to find she was penniless, Tamsin hadn't stayed longer than necessary before escaping to the relative peace and anonymity of France. Now it looked as if it might all open up again. Her father would become the butt of everybody's contempt. It looked as if she was the only one able to defend his memory. All she had to do was ask Jake Newman one thing. It seemed little enough. Emile must want Golden Boy an awful lot to go to such lengths to persuade her. And what had she got to lose?

'If I fail?' she demurred.

'You won't. I have great faith in your powers of persuasion.' He took her by the arm. 'Let's talk about it over dinner this evening. Yes?'

CHAPTER TWO

WHAT eventually transpired over dinner with Emile was that, as well as offering the stick, Emile contrived to offer the carrot as well—he promised Tamsin he would help her in her show-jumping career when she returned to France. Unsure whether to believe him or not, but unwilling to risk having her father's name dishonoured, she reluctantly agreed to try her powers of persuasion on Jake Newman. Now she had at last met him, she realised she had probably bitten off more than she could chew.

It was several days after that first ill-starred meeting when they met up again. This time she was surprised to find that his attitude had changed in some subtle way, and she wondered if he'd had a word with Saul. He surprised her by asking her if she would come over and work some of the horses with him one morning.

Even though it was still February, the fields were already clothed in spring green, as sparse as the hair on a baby's head, and the short turf of the gallops sparkled like emeralds in the early morning sunlight. It was beautiful countryside, and Jake's father owned several thousand acres of it. The house at the heart of it all was a classically proportioned Georgian mansion set like a jewel amid rolling parkland. There were breathtaking views of lavender-tinted hills on all sides, and a long avenue of beeches giving instant access to the bypass and the

M4. It was an ideal location for someone who did as much travelling as Jake.

As they rode slowly through a dripping copse, she was glad she was here exercising the horses with Jake rather than at her job in France. Her heart felt full of an inexplicable joy at the freshness of the morning, the gleaming thoroughbreds, and at the sight of Jake himself riding beside her on Golden Boy. He was bare-headed, and his black hair lifted and fell as he moved along.

So far they hadn't had a chance to talk. He always seemed so busy, and now it seemed as if he didn't want to break the heavy silence of the countryside that pressed around them. But eventually something seemed to encourage him to relax, and when he reached the edge of the open field he reined in, giving her a quizzical smile as she rode up behind him.

'The tempo of life here must be difficult to adjust to,' he began when she was in earshot. 'It must be quite a change from Chantilly.'

'It is,' she agreed, reining in her bay beside him.

He shot her an amused glance. 'Did you get on with him all right?'

'Who?' she arched her brow.

'De Monterrey, of course. Did you manage to keep him in his place?'

She felt herself blush. 'There were about seventy stable-girls,' she told him, when it dawned on her what he was getting at. 'And he's quite old; at least forty-five.'

'From what I've heard, he thinks he still has a certain allure for young girls. Especially beautiful ones. You mean to say you never had any problems with him?'

'I hardly ever met him,' she hedged, flooded with guilty feelings and imagining he could read her very thoughts. She urged her horse forward so as to avoid the all-seeing probing of his eyes. She felt as guilty as if what he was hinting at were true.

He caught up with her, as if determined not to let her get away, and began to canter easily along beside her again.

'How long were you working for him?' he probed.

'Six months,' she replied abruptly, wishing he would drop the subject. 'His manager offered me a job shortly after father died. It was a life-saver,' she felt moved to explain. 'Dad didn't leave anything but a tangle of debts and tax problems, as you probably heard ... He could manage horses all right, but he hadn't a clue about money, except how to enjoy it.'

She noticed the surprise on his face and his glance swept briefly over her well-cut jodhpurs and expensive leather boots, but, noticing the bitterness in her voice, too, he said, 'You look as if you've managed well enough. Money isn't everything.'

'It certainly helps!' Then she added, 'I've had this argument hundreds of times with the girls I roomed with in Chantilly. They seemed quite happy being treated as servants, so long as they could work on the glamorous fringes of the horse world.'

'But you're not?'

She shot him a green-eyed glance.

'No, you're not!' he interpreted with a smile.

'Would you be happy on a pittance, mucking out other people's horses? Half of them don't know one end from the other.'

'You had everything as a child, that's the trouble with you,' he told her casually. 'You're finding it difficult to have to live like everybody else for once.'

'How do you know what I was like as a child?' she asked curiously. And when he didn't answer she went on, 'You haven't a clue what it's like having to rely on other people to ask me to ride.' She shot him a glance. 'And that's only the half of it. Can you imagine how fed up I am with having to make do with last year's clothes all the time?'

He laughed. But she went on, 'When everybody found I wasn't the heiress they imagined, the partying stopped overnight.' She broke off, feeling tears threaten. It wasn't the parties. It was Dad. When he had died, she had suddenly found herself alone. But she couldn't tell Jake that yet. He was still a stranger. And the last thing she wanted was pity.

'Did the parties have to stop?' he asked, sounding surprised.

She dashed a hand across her face and pretended to adjust the buckle on her horse's reins. 'You wouldn't understand,' she muttered. 'How could I pretend to be in the same league with all the people I've grown up with when in reality I'm a pauper? I've no wish to be a hanger-on. I've got to make my own way now. It's not as easy as it looks.'

'So that's why you're back here and working with Saul? You're looking for a way back into show-jumping?'

'Yes,' she admitted slowly, 'I suppose I am.' It was partly true. The idea had been in her head ever since Saul had been so encouraging that first night back. And she could hardly admit the real reason to Jake himself. It *is* true, she told herself. Turning to him she said candidly, 'I feel so wretched. I don't want to be a failure. Dad expected me to do so well as a show-jumper——' She broke off with a sigh. 'But maybe I should stop dreaming and accept that it's all over——'

'But you can't?'

Her eyes filled with tears at the memory of her father's gruff faith in her. He had encouraged her and supported her and taught her all he knew. And now it had come to nothing. The thought came into her head that if only Jake would sell Golden Boy to Emile she would be able to make a fresh start.

Jake was smiling down at her. 'If this is you as a failure, I'm not complaining.'

'Well, I am!' she admitted. 'I can't help wanting to compete in top events again. Dad believed I was as good as anybody else. Better,' she added as an afterthought, giving him a shy smile. 'I would never be able to live with myself if I didn't keep faith with him.'

'It's tough at the top, Tammy. I thought you would have known that better than anyone——'

'I don't care about that! I could cope.'

Suddenly he gave her one of his dazzling smiles, and Tamsin realised that when he looked at her like that she liked him very much indeed, despite the fact that he would probably go on refusing to sell Golden Boy and she wouldn't earn her commission and Emile would change his mind about helping her to start up again.

She smiled across at him, happier than she would have thought possible, given all her problems. It was enough just to be with him.

As they rode along he kept the conversation light, telling her a little about his three months in America when he had ridden in several major competitions. And before long the inevitable happened, as she had known it would, and he mentioned Golden Boy.

Staring straight ahead, she took a deep breath and asked, 'You talk as if he is your principal hope?'

'That's right.'

Her heart sank but, realising that the time to ask the big question was here, she forced her voice to sound as casual as possible, and then asked, 'What about selling him if you got a good offer, Jake? Would you consider it?'

'Why, who's interested?' he shot back unexpectedly. The atmosphere seemed suddenly charged, and his earlier friendliness turned to a cold scrutiny.

'A lot of people,' she forced herself to go on as lightly as possible, 'aren't they?'

'De Monterrey, for instance?' His tone was ice.

Tamsin averted her face, blushing to the roots of her red-gold hair. 'I don't know,' she muttered.

'I wouldn't sell a rocking-horse to a man like that,' he clipped.

When she dared to look across at him he was still watching her. She glanced at Boy. 'I can see why you love him—he's magnificent,' she admitted, adding candidly, 'I would never be able to part with him, either.'

And that's that, she thought, bemused. Wheeler-dealer of the year! But it was a great load off her shoulders to know she didn't have to go any further with Emile's scheme. Faced with the reality of it, it now seemed tawdry even to have considered it. And, now Jake had said no, that was that. She would report back immediately. But then what? Would Emile give up so easily? She hated the thought of returning to Chantilly. And what if he still went ahead with his threat to drag her father's name through the mud? What if he guessed she hadn't really tried?

'Boy's got a couple of good years left in him,' Jake was telling her as he rode slightly on ahead as the track through the wood began to narrow. 'After that he'll be valuable at stud. That's the thing that makes him so interesting to people like de Monterrey. He'll be worth his weight in gold very shortly. Of course, as far as competing is concerned, by the time he's no longer showable another horse will be top and there'll be others coming up to take his place.'

He reined in at the top of the track and waited for her to draw level. 'Saul's training schedule will give me plenty of choice for the future. Oh,' he lifted his head, 'and yours, of course, if you decide to stay long.'

Tamsin had only registered half of what he was saying, but now, catching his drift, she immediately thought of the plan to return to France as soon as she had an answer. At the same moment she was registering Emile's promise to help her start up again for what it was—a cheap piece of manipulation aimed at getting her to do what he wanted.

'I'd love to stay,' she admitted, 'but there are difficulties.' She gave him a wry smile. 'The main one being, I haven't been asked!' She was surprised when Jake took her reply at face value.

'I would ask you,' he told her seriously, 'but it's a long-term commitment, and I can't imagine a husband of yours wanting to share you with the job. Half the year I'm out of the country and the other half I'm travelling between events at home. I expect my trainer to travel with me as Saul now does.'

'Marriage is the last thing on my mind,' she assured him.

'And if it came into conflict with your work?'

'I'll cross that bridge when I get to it,' she answered carefully. 'But surely the same problem faces you, too? Or do you only date girls who won't mind staying at home by themselves for half the year when they're married?'

'As you said, I'll cross that bridge when I get to it.' He chuckled. 'Right now I have no intention of getting caught in the marriage trap. I work hard. I play hard. And I make no commitments.'

Riding back underneath the trees on the edge of the wood, she reached up and trailed her fingers through the tracery of hanging branches. 'You could always marry somebody in the same game, who would want to travel with you,' she mused.

His harsh laugh pulled her up short.

'What have I said?' She looked at him in astonishent.

'If that's the direction your thoughts are straying, stop now,' he told her drily.

She could only stare. Then it dawned on her what he had mistakenly assumed from her casual remark. Her cheeks bloomed pink. He actually imagined she was putting herself forward as a marriage prospect! And after what she had just said, too. The idea was embarrassing and she didn't know how to respond. It couldn't have been further from the mark, either, for it had been his horse she had originally set out to get, not his ring!

As they began to wend their way back under the trees, ducking their heads beneath the branches, he returned to the topic in a rather roundabout way. 'If you're seriously thinking of getting back into show-jumping,' he told her, 'you'll need a hell of a lot of finance. Your best bet *would* be to marry into money.' He paused and gave her one of his smiles. 'It's a pity I'm not ready to put on the hand-cuffs, isn't it?'

He kicked his horse forward, and Tamsin watched as he began to gallop it down the length of the ride. That was a clear enough warning, she told herself wryly. And his determination not to sell Golden Boy had been clear enough, too.

All in all, she judged as she rode back to the stables after him, she had been a complete wash-out that morning. But she smiled. It didn't matter one bit. Emile couldn't prove she hadn't done her utmost to charm a 'yes' out of Jake. And it was heaven enough just being with him, whether marriage was on the cards or not.

CHAPTER THREE

HAPPY though she was to feel she no longer had to keep up any pretences, Tamsin still felt frightened to imagine Emile's reaction when she finally let him know her mission had been unsuccessful. The fear that he might still make public the letters allegedly concerning her father was uppermost, and she realised now, too late, that she should have demanded to see them and forced a promise from him to destroy them as soon as she had tried to do as he asked.

It was this uncertainty that led her to delay getting in touch with him right away; then, before she could do so, a letter arrived from France. She recognised his handwriting at once.

On opening it, she was dismayed to find a wad of bank notes inside. 'A little something on account, *ma belle*,' said the accompanying letter in Emile's spidery scrawl. 'Don't rush things,' he went on. 'I need that horse.'

Angry with herself for getting involved, and now even more angry that she hadn't taken the bull by the horns and extricated herself at the earliest opportunity, she now also felt thoroughly scared of the consequences, for what if Emile decided to turn nasty when she told him she was opting out? Feeling compromised, she stuffed the notes back into their envelope, hid the whole lot in a box on her dressing-table and wondered what to do next.

I'll think about it properly when I've got over the shock, she told herself, at a loss as to which way to turn. He says, don't rush. Well, I won't.

Her mind was taken off the problem to some extent by activities at Brantingham. As a celebrity, Jake was always being interviewed for this or that magazine, and later that same morning he asked Tamsin to come back at three o'clock. When she arrived, curious to know the reason for this summons—afternoons were always free—he was immaculately kitted out in full show-jumping gear. And he wasn't alone.

A glamorous-looking woman was peering intently through a camera lens when she arrived, while the object of her attentions sat astride Golden Boy and attempted to keep the highly strung jumper still for a moment. Tamsin soon learned that the camera-woman was an ex-fashion-model. She gave instructions for Tamsin to hold Boy's head until the crucial moment, and she then had to quickly snatch her hands away while the shot was taken.

An assistant, a girl in her late teens, evidently new to the job and still dazzled by the glamour of it all, chatted to Tamsin as the two stood and watched the rest of the session.

'I don't follow horses myself,' she confessed, 'and when Bianca said we were off to the country to take pics of gee-gees I nearly died.' She glanced down at her new, bright green gum boots. 'She sent me out to buy boots for us both and charge it to expenses—plus jackets and the Hermès headscarf she's wearing herself. Are you his girlfriend?' she went on, all in one breath.

Tamsin wished the girl would keep her voice down. 'Certainly not,' she answered shortly, giving a sidelong glance at Jake. His face twitched and she could tell he had overheard.

'He's quite a pin-up, isn't he?' Annie rattled on obliviously. 'I never realised tight white breeches and red coats could look so sexy! He must be rolling in it, too. What with this fabulous house and grounds, and all these horses!' She rummaged in one of the camera bags and triumphantly dragged out what she was looking for. 'Of course, we travel all over, snapping celebs. Bianca's freelance. She's beautiful, isn't she? I can just imagine her living in a place like this.'

Tamsin had to admit, Bianca was attractive—if you went for that over-blonde, heavily fake-tanned look, as Jake evidently did! Sliding down from the saddle, he moved over to Bianca, trailing the reins in one hand and bending his head as he said something to her. It made her laugh. Tamsin couldn't see that there was any need for her to look up into Jake's eyes with quite that besotted expression on her face. He wasn't that wonderful, was he? Of course, she'd known he would be attractive to other women, but it was disturbing to have such blatant evidence.

'We're just going up to the house for a few indoor shots.' He thrust Golden Boy's reins into her hands as he spoke. 'Give him a rub down when you put him back in the stall, will you?' He turned back to Bianca and they started to walk towards the house. Tamsin smarted at being dismissed like a stable-hand, until, gloomily, she accepted that that was all she was these days.

'See you!' called Annie cheerfully as, loaded with cameras, she shadowed Jake and Bianca across the terrace to the house.

I wonder how he'll make out with Annie dogging his steps, thought Tamsin with a grim smile.

Jake appeared in the yard just as Tamsin emerged from giving the horses their evening feed. The bright blue Manta with Bianca at the wheel had left only about five minutes ago. Tamsin had muttered to Lin as they did their rounds together that she'd thought Bianca and Annie were staying the night. Now Jake, looking handsome in white stock, tight breeches and shiny, knee-high leather riding-boots, with his hunting pink draped casually over one shoulder, came sauntering towards them both, an amused smile all over his clean-cut features.

'Thanks for helping out, Tamsin. If I'd known she was bringing an assistant, I wouldn't have taken up your afternoon.'

'No bother,' she began.

He was still smiling, 'Well, thank the lord for chaperons, anyway.'

'You mean to say you wanted protecting from Bianca?' she gave him a derisive glance. 'How conceited!'

'Not at all,' he protested. 'We had a brief run-in earlier this year. But luckily she seems easily discouraged.'

'Not by me——' she began.

He broke in, 'No, I heard you disclaim a romantic connection. Next time maybe you won't be so vehement?'

She folded her arms. 'Jake Newman, you may not be bad-looking, but it doesn't follow that every girl you come across is going to throw herself all over you. I'm sure Bianca has hordes of men chasing her——'

'I'm sure she has—but, like me, she prefers to do the chasing herself.'

'Oh, I see, birds of a feather. Maybe you should think twice about putting her off?' She paused.

'You don't understand, Tammy——'

'Don't call me that. What don't I understand?'

'Since I became quite well-known——' he spread his hands apologetically '—I seem to be a target for all the scalp-hunters in the country. Unlike you, they don't accept it when I say I'm not interested in anything permanent.' He grimaced. 'I suppose it's because they've seen me on TV. They go for the aura of fame—I could be a two-headed monster for all the difference it makes!'

Tamsin laughed aloud. He was anything but! Yet he looked so genuinely perplexed that, to her amazement, she felt a sudden desire to hug him. He seemed so sweet and confused, it was an effort to restrain the impulsive gesture.

'You mean, like teenagers chasing pop stars?'

He nodded. 'Or tennis-court groupies... Why do they do it, Tam?'

She gave him a long-suffering look. 'Poor Jake. I wonder why! I must say, though, my heart bleeds for you. It must be really tough at the top!'

He gave her one of his breath-stoppers, a dazzle of even white teeth in the tanned, clean-cut face. 'I'm not saying it doesn't have its compensations!' He chuckled wickedly, then took her by the hand. 'Promise me something, Tammy—promise you'll stick around whenever necessary? I'll feel safer with you there to ward them off!'

She hid her annoyance, not overjoyed that he saw her as some sort of minder.

'All you have to do is act decorative and possessive... please?' He gave her a 'little boy' look.

Maybe redheads weren't his type, after all? Biting back her own feelings on the matter, she injected a mischievous note into her voice, asking, 'Will I get an Oscar?'

'It depends how convincing you are——' His dark eyes adopted a sudden suggestive glint.

Lin had disappeared by now and they were alone, standing just inside the stable door. Without either of them changing position, Jake's arm slid around her waist. 'You've got a fabulous body—these tight-fitting jodhpurs look sensational on you. Have you ever thought of taking up modelling?'

'Do me a favour!' Her attempted brashness fell flat as the touch of his hand lightly traced the shape of her hips and brought a sharp intake of breath from her. She tried to slide out of range, but her limbs refused to do as she wanted and his fingers rippled up her spine until they reached the nape of her neck. Gently he brought her face closer to his own. There was a long moment while his lips hovered above hers.

It was her chance to draw back, but while she wavered, lost in the will-defeating nearness of his body, he lowered his head until his lips rested lightly on hers. Then the kiss deepened, gradually bringing with it a fiery confusion of emotion that left Tamsin breathless.

For a long moment afterwards his glance probed deeply into hers, then with painful slowness his hand slid from out of the tangle of red hair. As the contact was broken, she stepped hastily back out of reach.

'You shouldn't do that to complete strangers,' she choked, trying to say something that would put the kiss back in perspective. It surfaced with disturbing insistence, as if nothing would ever again seem quite the same.

'We're not strangers,' he responded softly, after a short pause in which he seemed to be searching for words. 'We're not strangers, Tamsin, not us.'

'We only met days ago,' she tried to say as he went on holding her within the encirclement of his arms. It felt strangely natural, as if she belonged there. His face was so close, she could see the flecks of gold and amber in his eyes.

'We met ages ago,' he insisted with a huskiness in his voice that brought an excited thrill to her soul.

'I don't believe you.' Her thoughts raced, and she tried to avoid his eyes in case she became convinced, and succumbed to his persuasion.

'We met in Shropshire,' he insisted. 'You were about ten.' He laughed softly.

Vaguely she recalled a long-forgotten pony-club show. He confirmed her guess.

'I was riding a new pony, a proper little devil as it turned out, though I dare say my riding had something to do with it, too.' He was still holding her, his voice still huskily charged with emotion.

'I don't remember *you*.'

He was standing too close, his arms warm and gentle, but his words were a welcome diversion from anything more dangerous.

'It's printed all too clearly on my mind, I'm afraid!' he went on, unaware of the chaos of her emotions.

'Why?' she asked, trying to make her voice sound normal, despite the strange things his touch was doing to her.

'My pony ran out at the first jump,' he told her, 'then he proceeded to demolish the rest of the course. When he came to the wall, I went over but he didn't. Believe me, there's nothing worse than leaving a show-ring minus the mount you set out with.'

'So where do I come in?' she managed to ask.

'You were waiting your turn on a very smartly turned-out little fellow. You wore your hair in two long plaits and had a haughty, perfect little oval of a face. When I came puffing up, covered in mud, you gave me a look that cut me to shreds. There and then I vowed to do better!'

'Our roles are reversed somewhat,' she muttered, achingly conscious of the hard, muscled body touching her own and making her knees feel weak and her mouth go horribly dry. 'I still don't remember you,' she told him, trying to sound brisk and oblivious to his touch.

'You wouldn't. Why should you? I was just another worm underfoot. Needless to say, you went on to win. I followed your career with interest after that.'

She broke into a smile, licking dry lips as she did so. 'I won a lot in those days—and I was probably frightened when I saw you come off...'

'More likely you thought I was an utter fool. I certainly felt like it!' He grinned disarmingly, but the lightness of tone belied the intensity in his eyes. She felt confused; it was as if he was on the brink of saying something else, and the feeling thrust her out of her depth and she floundered, longing to let him know she was nothing like that spoiled eight-year-old on the pony, but he moved even closer so that she found herself pressed back against the wooden partition separating two loose-boxes.

'So now you know why I feel justified in kissing you—we're not strangers at all.'

'It scarcely warrants——' she began, but the pressure of his lips stifled her protests and she found herself being rapidly swept up in a maelstrom of unexpected emotion as their bodies sought and found each other. A fleeting thought that he was her boss was followed at once by the recognition that it was heaven being kissed by him. She let his lips pressure hers, not caring about anything else just then.

'You're so lovely, Tamsin,' he murmured, lifting his lips for a moment and letting them tease their way down the side of her face and neck. When she peeped at him through lids now weighted with the languor of desire, the expression on his face made him look as if he was drinking her in, and the rest of him was proof of his sudden flare of desire. Being trapped in a corner by the boss was something that had almost happened before and, joking about it to her room-mates later, they had all had a good laugh over the incident. But now, faced with virtually the same scene, though with a very different man, she was seeing rainbows...melting... floating...

'I must be off my head,' she murmured against the side of his lean, tanned, faintly spice-scented skin. This was far more than she had bargained for.

'Why so?' he asked huskily, still intent on exploring every centimetre of her features with his lips.

'Allowing the boss to get me in a corner——'

'We may as well start as we mean to go on,' he countered, pulling her tighter to him, his voice so thick with desire that it excited her own desires, so that it was a shock to realise how thin the dividing

line was between common sense and complete
abandon.

From somewhere she managed to summon up the
will to say, 'I'm not like this, Jake. Let me go...'

'Go?' He looked astonished. 'Go where?'

'Just away. Stop touching me.'

He looked bewildered. 'Stop touching you?'

'Of course. I don't want you to touch me.'

He gave his famous smile. 'I get it—it's games
time...' As if to underline what he thought, he ran
a hand down her spine, bringing her to a state where
she thought she might easily burst into flames.
'Later?' he murmured thickly, drawing her briefly
back into his arms, then moving away.

She was confused to see how easily he could let
her go. As if his kisses and caresses had been a
practice session, not the real thing at all. He noticed how rapidly she was breathing, and reached
out to take her face between his two hands.

'We're going to be so good together, Tammy.
You're sensational.'

'You're on the wrong track altogether, Jake, and
will you please not call me Tammy?'

His face crumpled into a smile. 'Marmalade any
better? The girl with the marmalade hair...'

She had flattened herself as far back against the
wooden partition as she could and, putting her
hands up to his, she pulled them down from her
face and gave him one of her haughtiest stares. 'I
have no intention of tumbling into the hay with you.
I don't see that as part of my duties.'

'That's the look,' he said. 'That's the one I remember. Worms of the world unite, you have
nothing to do but be squashed.' Then, more seriously, he said, 'You think you mean it, don't you?'

She nodded.

'Looks like yours and a body screaming out for me, and you say you don't see it as part of your duties? Kitten,' he went on, 'if it's any consolation, I don't see it as part of your duties, either. I see it as a force of nature. We want each other—at least, the bits of us do that haven't been trampled into oblivion by convention.' He paused, and for a moment she thought he was going to kiss her again, but instead he said slowly, 'So now, what are we going to do about it? Nothing?'

His whole manner told her he had absolutely no intention of doing nothing, but so far she had been unable to interrupt. Now all she could do was repeat what she had already said, as if she had found a life-line. 'I don't want you to touch me.' Her voice sounded smoky, and she turned her head so she couldn't see that fabulous smile. Jake didn't move, but the space between them seemed charged with the tangible electricity of his presence.

'It's only lust, after all,' she managed to say weakly.

'Yeah, yeah, only lust. So what's so bad about lust?' he rasped with a sudden edge to his voice.

'I don't sleep around——'

'Please don't say "with just anybody", or I'll burst into tears.' He grinned disarmingly. 'I thought it was OK to sleep around these days if you felt like it? I thought that's what women's lib was all about?'

'I think we also say we're free to say no——'

'Even when you'd rather say yes?'

'But I wouldn't——'

'Don't deceive yourself.'

'No—I—it would be a meaningless physical exercise, wouldn't it?' she flashed.

A look dawned in his eyes. 'Do you mean what I think you mean? It would be meaningless without a ring?'

Her eyes widened.

'That's the picture, is it?' Suddenly his eyes lost their bantering look. 'Same old scenario. So what's new? I think I've already told you I do my own chasing. I'm primitive like that.' He moved a little away and the electric tension between them seemed to slacken. 'You're too beautiful to treat like one of the boys, Tamsin, but marriage is definitely out. If you don't want a repeat performance of this little scene, I suggest you get out.'

Her heart stopped. 'Get out?'

He sighed. 'I'm not giving you the sack! You're an insecure one, aren't you? Do you think I'd sack a girl because she wouldn't leap into the hay with me? Thanks a lot!' His expression became gentler. 'I don't know why you're so worried about losing your job here, but I'll have a contract written out if that's what's bothering you, OK?'

Relief overwhelmed her once more, and she let him take her hand. All traces of his former desire seemed firmly under control. 'What did you mean by *getting out*?' she asked.

'I meant out of harm's way—into a nunnery or something. There'll always be men wanting you, and you're going to have to learn to cope with it.' He held her glance for a moment. 'For the record, I don't see what I feel for you as merely one of the perks of the job...I'd want to take you to bed wherever we'd met.'

She blushed violently at his outspokenness, and she could tell from the gleam of satisfaction in his eyes that he'd noticed. He also registered the trembling of her fingers in his. 'I could be a real cynical devil and tell you that I'll be happy to play a waiting game. It could give a man a sadistic pleasure to watch you reach breaking point——' Sensuously trailing a hand over her hips, he pressured her close against his hard, aroused body, encased in the tight, white riding breeches. She felt a flare of desire rocket through her.

'How long do you think you can hold out, angel?' he murmured in her ear.

His confidence threatened to overwhelm her, but she prised his arm from around her waist and gave him the look again. 'You'll need the patience of Job,' she said with a tight smile, 'and then some!'

Feeling his eyes smouldering through her, she walked out of the stables with as much nonchalance as she could muster.

Only when she was at last sitting behind the wheel of Saul's Lamborghini did she give vent to her true feelings. She thumped the steering-wheel with her fist. Could she stay at Brantingham after this? She was in a total muddle. There was no denying how attractive he was—he was a positive danger!—and she could scarcely hide from the devil himself how he got through to her. But he was open about being interested in only one thing, and she had no intention of getting into that sort of dead-end affair—no matter how enticing he seemed!

She put the car into gear and moved smoothly out of the yard without daring a glance in the rearview mirror.

On the short drive home her mind seethed like a battlefield. When she had first agreed to come here it had been qualms about earning Emile's commission that had worried her. Now there was a bigger worry. Not only had she thrown away her commission, she was in danger of throwing away something far more precious—her heart.

By the time she brought the car to a stop outside Rose Mead, she had made up her mind.

There was no way she could let herself be sidetracked by the wild, wayward enchantment of Jake Newman's smile. There was far too much at stake. She would give anything to get away—to put as much distance as possible between herself and the danger he represented—but she couldn't. So she would simply have to school herself to resist. Resist Jake Newman? She gave a hollow laugh. But he was danger, red-hot danger, and there was no other choice.

CHAPTER FOUR

THE WAD of notes from Emile had been lying in the box on top of her dressing-table for some days now. The more she looked at it, the more it seemed like a reproach.

Contrary to what she had expected, Jake was behaving like a perfect gentleman—waiting for her to break, she observed cynically to herself. But, whether by design or accident, they hadn't been alone together since that afternoon in the stables. She still burned with the memory, but firmly tried to shut it out of her mind, as if that would make it disappear forever.

As the days passed, she realised with fascination that she was undergoing some sort of sea-change. It wasn't as easy as she'd hoped to resist Jake's spell. Even the kid-glove treatment only seemed to add to his attraction. And instead of trying to take matters into her own hands, she began to wait passively for something to happen. She lived in hope that Emile would step in, telling her to let the whole matter of the purchase of Golden Boy drop, then suggesting that she might as well stay in England, after all. Secretly, of course, she knew she would have to bring herself to tell him she wanted out. But something, Jake himself, kept her in a state of passivity, waiting, waiting to see what would happen next. Waiting, perhaps, for his next kiss.

She actually managed to get as far as finding out when the post office in Market Appleby was open so she could arrange to have the money returned, but such was the fear that this would immediately bring her time at Brantingham to an end, she never quite seemed to get around to doing anything more. The days slid by.

One evening Jake decided to take the novices over to a nearby show. What with a stable of twenty horses and a punishing schedule of trials and training, Jake himself seemed to work all hours. Starting at six-thirty, he was often still busy till nine or ten at night. It was a surprise then when he turned to her as she took her place beside him in the Range Rover before starting out and asked, 'How about a spot of dinner tomorrow?'

'I was beginning to think you never took time off,' she replied lightly, her heart beginning to race.

'The folks are flying in from the Bahamas the next day for an overnight stop before going on to Madrid, and it's Badminton for me afterwards, so it may be the only chance we'll get.' He gave a wide smile at the prospect of a big event. 'We're rather short on French cuisine around here, but there's a pleasant little restaurant down by the riverside at Halsham, if you'd like that?'

'Sounds lovely,' Tamsin agreed. A burger take-away would have sounded lovely to her ears, so long as the invitation was issued from Jake's lips. She looked at them now. Firm and soft, they made her tingle with desire as she remembered what their touch did to her.

His strong face was outlined against an apricot sky as he drove along, and he had the breath-stopping glamour of a movie star, she thought, with that thick, dark hair and handsome, clean-cut profile. The bonus was, he seemed modestly un-aware of how special he was. His outdoors life had given his skin a perpetual glow of good health, and the dark eyes with their faint etching of laugh-lines at the corners were always provokingly alive, making him look as if he had ten times more vitality than any other man. It seemed an age since they had lazed over her body in that sensually explorative way, bringing her senses to life as nothing had ever done before. All her carefully erected defences were in ruins as they drove along in the golden haze of the February sun towards the show ground.

The novices performed well, and Tamsin longed to be out there in the ring with Jake, enjoying the applause of an enthusiastic crowd and the exhilaration of bringing on such lovely animals.

Afterwards Jake was keyed up, like an actor who has just come off stage after an especially thrilling performance.

He needs time to unwind, thought Tamsin tenderly, noting the thumb marks of fatigue beneath the dancing eyes.

'You drive yourself too hard,' she murmured in the privacy of the Range Rover later on. He didn't say anything, but the look he gave her made her stomach lurch at the depth of meaning in it. 'Have you ever considered taking somebody on to ride the novices for you?' she asked hurriedly. It was an abrupt question, one she had longed to broach, growing daily in importance the more she put off asking it.

'It certainly crosses my mind from time to time,' he replied non-committally.

She didn't dare glance up, but couldn't help murmuring, 'I'm always available.' If he would only say yes, it would give her an excuse to stay by his side for good.

'Are you, now?' He gave her a dry glance, quite different from previous ones. 'I'll remember that.' He started the Range Rover at once and she was saved the embarrassment of talking her way out of it just then.

When they reached the top of the lane leading down to Rose Mead, she suggested that he drop her off to save the extra few minutes. 'So you can get some rest,' she explained.

'Wouldn't hear of it,' he informed her. 'I'm not having you roaming about the countryside at night without an escort.'

A few minutes later the headlamps picked out the white wall of the house with the swags of clematis thatching the porch. An owl hooted distantly in the copse nearby.

'It's so lovely here,' sighed Tamsin. 'In fact, it's been a lovely evening all round. It's so good to be part of the scene again. I've missed it so much.'

'Not bored with England yet?' He raised an eyebrow.

'Bored? How could I be?'

He reached across to unlock her door, and she felt a mixture of relief and disappointment that he hadn't attempted to kiss her goodnight. Obviously he didn't intend to test her availability just yet!

'I thought you'd be missing the bright lights and sophistication of Chantilly,' he remarked casually.

'This life is glamorous enough for me,' she replied at once.

'Looking after other people's horses?' he queried, eyeing her carefully. 'I thought you had something more ambitious in mind?'

Just then a light came on in the porch. It was Saul, eager to find out how the novices had performed. While they talked, Tamsin made a plea of tiredness which wasn't far from the truth, and went indoors.

Despite the cloud represented by Emile, she fell asleep with a lingering feeling of contentment. Jake made simple things special.

When he arrived to pick her up next evening, Jake gave a low whistle, his glance roving in open appreciation all over her slim form in its claret silk two-piece. She was glad she'd gone to some trouble. She stood at the top of the stairs and smiled down at him. Prolonging the moment, she sauntered as slowly as she dared towards him, shocked to find she was enjoying his blatant appraisal so much. Please, she thought silently, don't let me ever have to go back to Chantilly!

His glance had dropped to her feet in their spiky-heeled patent shoes, hovering over the slim ankles with an expression of pleased surprise, then lingering like a caress over the fabulous legs in the fine black stockings. His gaze continued to hover at the hem of her skirt, as if he could lift it by the sheer power of the desire he was making no attempt to conceal, but then it moved on bit by bit up the curves of her body in its expensive silk sheath, so that by the time she descended to the bottom step and stood level with him their eyes met in a challenge of bright desire.

A brief goodnight to Saul led them out into the night. The air was warm and rain-scented, fragrant with flowers, and Tamsin shivered with expectation before slithering into the passenger seat beside him.

'I hope I'm going to be able to keep the pack at bay tonight,' he told her, his glance lingering on the deep V of her jacket. 'You look like a two-man job.'

'I'm sure you can manage without help,' she murmured, unable to avoid a suggestive huskiness in her tone.

'Yes, I usually do,' he remarked, eyeing her from the shadows.

Tamsin moistened her lips and glanced up at him through extravagant dark lashes. Jake was deliberately flirting with her, and he was making her melt with desire already!

'I think we'd better get a move on,' he said firmly, dragging his glance away from her upturned face and sending the car rapidly forwards into the lane.

Tamsin shivered as she observed the masterful way he swung the car into the traffic when they reached the main road. His air of authority warned her that it would be dangerous to let him think she was easy meat. He might just be the type not to take 'no' for an answer if things got too hot to handle. But he almost forced her to flirt with him by the lazy, humorous way he looked at her. It was a look designed to be provoking, and she was certainly provoked! She managed to keep silent for the rest of the journey, letting him lead the conversation, defusing the wildness of her reactions by concentrating on what he was telling her.

The restaurant was crowded when they arrived, and heads turned as they made their way to the intimate corner table reserved for them. A buzz of conversation showed Jake had been recognised. Tamsin was pleased she had gone to some trouble over her appearance. She flicked back a tendril of sherry-coloured hair and smiled up at him with her green cat's eyes.

'This is lovely, Jake.' She gave a glance at the stiff damask, the solid silver, the fine china, the trailing hot-house plants, appreciating the quiet air of luxury.

'I thought it might be your sort of place,' he replied ambiguously, holding her glance for a moment longer than necessary.

'So?' she asked, surprised at the look and wondering what it meant.

'So where do we start?' he demanded bluntly. His eyes lost their bantering expression and seemed to skewer her to the spot.

'I don't know what you mean!' she blurted. Despite her words, she blushed violently, suddenly imagining he knew all about Emile's designs on Golden Boy and her part in the scheme.

'I invited you here, Tamsin, not only for the pleasure of your company, but also in the hope we could lay our cards on the table.'

'In what way?' she mumbled, biting her lip, all her composure deserting her.

'Look, don't fool with me. I know what your ambitions are. I'm not totally stupid. And although we haven't met since you were ten—if that could be called a meeting—I've heard enough about you to know you're the ambitious type. Hell, you were all set to make it big—very big indeed. You're not seriously trying to tell me you've changed overnight into a stay-at-home?'

'You mean show-jumping?' The turn the conversation had taken confused her. It was so unexpected.

'What else?' He paused. 'Unless, of course, you had some other reason for getting yourself put on the payroll at Brantingham?'

She opened her mouth, then snapped it shut. It was obvious what other reason he imagined. They'd already done that one during their ride the other morning. 'I can assure you,' she began hotly, 'I'm not one of these husband-hunting females you're so afraid of. The very last thing I want is——'

'All right, all right. But you won't deny you want something out of me?'

He was both so near and so far from the truth, she blushed again in confusion, guilt vying with relief because he obviously didn't know the true reason for her guilty feelings.

'I thought as much,' he went on after a close scrutiny of her expression, before she could interrupt. 'So you're planning to ride the second string, impress me with your ability to win, then slowly take over the main bunch?' He gave a soft, musical laugh. 'What you haven't realised yet, Tamsin, is I don't like to be hustled, by anyone, not even a gorgeous, seductive, green-eyed . . .' His voice trailed away and he seemed to forget what he was going to say next, his eyes plunging into the depths of her soul, sending all other feelings except the one single, strong desire to be loved by this man right out of her head.

Before she could stutter a response, the waiter materialised at their table, and by the time he left Jake seemed to have pulled himself together, adding only, 'Lecture over. I wanted you to know where you stood, that's all.'

The evening was almost over before something was said that popped the question of riding for him, and thereby finding an excuse to stay at Brantingham, into her mind again. 'You're so set against me riding for you because you still think of me as ten. Well, I've improved somewhat since then, Jake. I really have!' She said it lightly, but his reply brought a frown.

'It's a hard world,' he told her. 'No room in it for mistakes or amateurs.'

'I was never an amateur,' she told him. Then, looking bleakly at her plate, she said, 'The answer really is no, isn't it? You don't want me around—except to muck out your horses.'

Instead of answering straight away, there was a pause. She raised eyes that were tear-sheened.

'Nothing's ever definite.' His voice thickened for some reason. 'What happens next surely depends on how desperate you are?'

The words hung between them; Tamsin felt her breath stop and she heard with unnatural clarity the sound of her own heartbeats and the random clatter of the busy restaurant. There could surely be no mistaking his meaning? And, what was clearer still, he was putting her dedication to the test.

In a flat voice she forced herself to say, 'To ride professionally is my sole ambition.'

There was a fraction of a pause. Jake's face didn't alter. His tawny eyes were for once almost lifeless. Then a corner of his mouth jerked. He asked, 'I suppose that means you'll go to any lengths?'

'Naturally,' she replied through frozen lips. 'Isn't that what dedication is?'

'I always like to know the rules of the game,' he told her with a brief, cold smile. 'At least it makes a change from being hunted down as a marriage prospect——' His glance was wary as it raked her expression.

Tamsin's hair prickled up the back of her neck. Sometimes Jake seemed psychic. If it wasn't exactly marriage she was after, it was something like it. She just wanted to be near him and dared not think any further ahead than that. But she wanted his respect too, and she couldn't see him getting seriously involved with a mere groom. Everything was very clear. If only he would do as she wanted and let her ride for him, he would eventually find he needed her by his side forever.

But what had she done, letting him think she would do anything to further her ambitions?

CHAPTER FIVE

JAKE intercepted her just as she was lugging a bale of straw out of the store early the next morning. Without any sort of greeting, he said, 'I want you to take Golden Boy and Chelsea over a few jumps in the school this afternoon while I pick the folks up from the airport.'

Before she could say anything he turned and went back towards the house. He had a self-contained apartment in a wing of the house, and Tamsin watched as he skirted the railings and strode off towards it. He looked quite different from the groomed escort of the previous evening—an old khaki sweater replacing the dinner-jacket, baggy brown cords over short jodhpur boots completing his get-up—but he still looked infuriatingly attractive, like a little boy with that rumpled black hair, and even more endearing—and still, more than anything, dangerously untouchable to a girl with any sort of heart.

Tamsin had mixed feelings about his unexpected offer. It was quite a turnabout after what he had said the previous evening, and she shuddered to think he might seriously expect to collect. That was not the sort of relationship she wanted to stay around for—even though, when he smiled deeply into her eyes as if she were the only woman in the world, she thought even that would be better than nothing.

All thought of exerting her obviously useless powers of persuasion on behalf of Emile had faded into oblivion. If she kept quiet, maybe he would even forget he had ever suggested the idea that had brought her to Brantingham. Out of sight, out of mind, she prayed. Still she hadn't returned his 'little bit on account', but she intended to do it any day now.

More important was the challenge of that afternoon. Only if she proved herself would she feel justified in trying to persuade Jake to let her stay on.

In the solitude of the indoor school, she eventually put the horses and herself through their paces. She was disappointed that Jake wasn't there to watch, but all that was forgotten when, flushed and exhilarated, she at last led the horses back to their stalls.

Returning to Rose Mead, she flung herself into a chair opposite Saul and gave him a beatific smile.

'I can see you're pleased with yourself,' he remarked, smiling at her over a mug of tea.

'Not so much with myself,' she smiled, 'but certainly with those two. I guess I could ride either of them against some pretty stiff competition and not disgrace either them or myself. They're both wonderful. Jake's a very lucky devil.'

'Aye, he's got a good eye for horse flesh. And he's going to be dead chuffed you got on well with his little darlings. But,' he went on, 'he's a man who likes to see for himself.'

Tamsin went upstairs to change.

On her dressing-table she rediscovered the wad of bank notes in the torn envelope into which she had first thrust them. She fingered the money thoughtfully. The sooner it was safely on its way, the better. She could only hope Emile wouldn't turn out to be the snake he threatened. His threat seemed very distant now, and it was an effort to remember why she had taken him so seriously.

When Jake came back later with his people, she and Saul went up to the house to have a drink with them. They were, as Jake had already told her, only touching down for the night before flying on to Madrid, where the Colonel was to judge some international dressage championships. Saul too was leaving next day for a holiday with some old racing friends in Ireland.

Badminton was a seething mass of spectators, and Olley, cursing the traffic all the way down, had difficulty in finding a decent space for the horse-box. Jake, despite an early night, looked strangely drawn, as if he had something weighty on his mind, and Tamsin felt shut out when he refused to talk.

To add to this, Lin chatted non-stop all the way down about her sister's new baby and the romper suit she was knitting her—so that with the three of them she soon felt like screaming. Jake, she decided, must be a bundle of nerves. That was why he scarcely looked at her, and why he nearly bit her head off when she asked him if he wanted a cup of coffee.

Chelsea was tacked up as soon as they arrived, and Jake vaulted into the saddle, telling everybody to keep a close eye on Golden Boy before edging out into the crowd, half of whom shouldn't have been in the enclosure anyway. While he took Chelsea over the practice jumps, they all took it in turns to go off and have a look around. Tamsin was surprised they took his order to watch Golden Boy so seriously.

Olley was evasive when she asked the reason. 'Taking no chances, is he?' He didn't lift his head. The shut-out feeling came back.

When it was her own turn to take a look round, she wended her way between the booths selling riding kits and Scotch rugs and leather saddles, until she eventually found herself standing before a display of sheepskin coats. She was just running her fingers appreciatively over the soft skin when a voice at her elbow spoke up. Turning, she found a man in a tweed cap beside her.

'One of Newman's crowd, are you?' he asked pleasantly. She nodded, surprised he should know that.

'Tamsin Harland?' he asked with a discreet lowering of his voice and a quick glance from side to side. Thinking he must be one of her father's old acquaintances, she nodded, and he said, 'I have something for you, from our mutual friend.'

'From whom?'

She watched in sudden trepidation as he felt inside his jacket and drew from it a bulky white envelope. 'Open it somewhere private,' he advised as he quickly slipped it into her hand. Then, before she could question him, he moved off out of sight behind a row of jackets, and by the time she followed him he was already mingling with the crowd on the far side of the main avenue.

Curiosity to see what was in the envelope gave way to foreboding, and, making her way rapidly across the grass to the toilet tents, she ducked inside, tied the flap securely behind her, then tore open the envelope with shaking fingers.

Inside was a neatly typed letter. It was from Emile. Scanning it, she blanched at the contents. He mentioned that he had already paid her an advance for her expected help and now she would find enclosed a further five hundred pounds and the contents of a plastic bag.

Fingers trembling, she unfolded the rest of the letter and stared at the small bag that had been concealed within the pages. Even without opening it she could see that it contained two tablets—or rather, horse pills, she corrected, remembering the times she had watched the vet administer similar ones to her father's occasionally ailing animals.

Shudders of fear hurdled up and down her spine. Emile must know she wouldn't agree to anything illegal, or harmful to the horse, come to that. So how dared he presume to involve her in this way? She gazed at the letter as if willing it to vanish into thin air, then forced herself to read on. She could hear Emile's voice, his precise, inflected English, in every word.

Judging by the silence from Brantingham, Mr Newman was being uncooperative about the sale of Golden Boy, she read. Other methods must therefore be used where friendly persuasion had failed. Frankly, he went on, he was surprised she had had so little success, and felt he ought to remind her of certain complications if matters did not turn out well. Now, he went on, it was time to administer the enclosed at intervals of twelve hours, the first to be given the day after their return from Badminton. She should have no qualms as the dose was harmless, but it might just convince Jake Newman that Golden Boy was not worth hanging on to.

She re-read the letter, fingered the bank notes as if she could make them disappear, then noticed a PS on the reverse of the single sheet. It reminded her that ten per cent would be paid into her account on receipt of the bill of sale from the Newman stables.

Cursing her own stupidity at getting involved with such a scheme, she stuffed the tablets back into the envelope, together with the money and Emile's letter, and considered throwing it all into the toilet. Thinking better of it, she buried it in the pocket of her Barbour.

She would give the whole lot to Jake. He would know what to do. The time for struggling on alone against Emile was over. Jake would surely understand that her father could never have been involved in anything underhand. Saul would bear that out. And together they could help her protect her father's name from Emile's malice. Feeling that at last she was being sensible, she emerged from the tent.

It was raining.

She tramped all the way round the show-ring, heading back towards the box, without getting a glimpse of Jake.

When she neared their pitch she saw he was already back. Golden Boy was being led down the ramp, and she was surprised to notice he was still wearing his head-collar and the navy blue and red blanket with Jake's initials scrolled in the corners.

Everybody was standing around with their eyes on the horse. Even from a distance she could see Jake looked pale. In fact, he looked almost grey with what could only be described as cold rage, she realised as she came closer. The letter in Tamsin's pocket burned like a coal.

Rain was pounding on the van roof now, with a sound like stampeding horses. Golden Boy on the contrary was quiet, almost docile, and when Jake dropped the leading rein he didn't walk off as he usually did, but stood with drooping head and half-shut eyes.

'He likes the rain as little as we do,' Tamsin said to break the silence that hung over the group as she came up.

Jake gave her a look of speechless fury. Rain was already plastering his black hair to his skull. 'Get him back in the box, Olley. You——' he swung on Tamsin '—you're coming with me.'

Giving her no time to protest, he lunged forward and, gripping her by the wrists, dragged her off in the direction of the huddled wooden buildings that housed the officials of the course.

'But aren't you due in the ring any minute?' she panted as he dragged her roughly over the turf.

'Riding what?' he bit out. Only when they reached the relative shelter of the wooden office where the chairman officiated did he speak again, but it was only to say, 'I hope you've got a damned good story worked out.'

Fear blanched her features. 'What—what do you mean? I——' Just then the door opened and someone came out of the office, and it gave Jake the opportunity to push her in ahead of him. They stood, the two of them, dripping rain all over the wooden floor, as a burly, military-looking man looked up from behind a desk.

Tamsin held her breath, waiting for Jake to launch into his accusations.

'I'm scratching Golden Boy,' she heard him say. He paused long enough to give her a fright, then said, 'He's off form.'

'Pity. I was looking forward to seeing him win.' The chairman made a mark on a list. 'Anything serious?'

'It could well be.' Jake's tones were ominous. Tamsin held her breath at what was to come. To her surprise he gripped her wrist and, without any further explanations, marched her outside into the rain once more.

When they were in the lee of the hut, he dragged her up against him. Waves of relief were sweeping through her, but they were short-lived.

'Thank your lucky stars there's no hard proof at this stage. You're off the hook for the moment.'

Tamsin shivered as she found herself exposed to his laser-like scrutiny. 'Don't look at me like that. I haven't done anything.'

'Don't play the innocent with me, darling,' he warned, his voice heavy with disgust.

'I don't know what you mean.'

'Then I'll spell it out. Golden Boy has been doped.'

Her sharp intake of breath was spontaneous and made him pause. 'I don't know anything about it——' she began to protest in a frightened voice. That much was true. It didn't have to be Emile who had doped Golden Boy this time, did it? But, even as the thought flashed through her mind, she knew she was deceiving herself.

Her words, however, seemed to cast a sliver of a doubt in Jake's own mind.

'Isn't it just too much of a coincidence?' he demanded through gritted teeth. 'His reputation? The fact that he's admitted he wants that horse? And for six months you were in his pay. Still are, yes?' He fingered her neck. 'It would be crass of him to get you to slip something into Boy's feed, I admit that, but I wouldn't put it past a snake like him.'

'Do you really think I'd do a thing like that?' she demanded in real fury, grabbing his sleeve.

'Let's just say you're on probation. One suspicious move and I'll know you're in it up to your beautiful neck.'

She found her arms curving around him, dragging him close as if to force him to listen. 'I had nothing to do with it, Jake. Please believe me,' she told him urgently. It seemed the most important thing in the world that he shouldn't think ill of her.

For a moment they rocked there together in the rain like two lovers. Then Jake shook himself free from her grasp. 'Don't try that method on me, sweetheart. I told you, I don't like it.'

The way his body had melted against hers for an instant seemed to belie his words, but before she could pull herself together Jake was spinning abruptly on his heels and ploughing through the crowd with a complete disregard for good manners.

'Jake!' called Tamsin. But when he didn't turn back she knew it was for the best. For what could she tell him? That, despite his suspicions and, worse, despite the contents of the letter in her pocket, she had never, ever agreed to go this far in Emile's scheme? Would Jake believe her? She trembled to take the risk.

When she reached the horse-box a few minutes later, Olley was already behind the wheel, with Lin beside him.

'Where's Jake?' she asked, looking round.

'In the back with the horses,' replied Olley shortly.

'Is Golden Boy going to be all right?' she asked nervously as she climbed up on to the driving bench.

'Let's all hope so.' Olley's face was expressionless.

Lin leaned across when Tamsin was settled in beside her. 'They love that horse,' she whispered beneath the whine of the engine. 'He and Jake will be up all night with him.' She looked puzzled. 'I thought he was just a bit under the weather. I never dreamed somebody would deliberately poison him. It's a rotten thing to do.'

'Hateful,' agreed Tamsin with genuine fervour. Lin's words stabbed her with a dreadful guilt. If she hadn't been so weak in the first place, allowing herself to be bullied into going along with Emile, then later letting things slide as she herself slid deeper under Jake's spell, she might have been able to stop this whole thing before it took the turn it had.

It was a nightmare journey back. The drumming rain through which Olley drove the huge van with reckless haste emphasised the heavy silence within. The three of them were occupied with their own thoughts. If Golden Boy died, worried Tamsin, too scared to mention such a possibility aloud, what then?

When they got back, Jake told Lin to get some rest after the other horses had been made comfortable. Olley fretted around Boy's stall like a nanny with a sick child, while Jake mixed some concoction or other in the tack-room.

'You'd better come and watch,' he told Tamsin. As if to spare her nothing, he insisted she help Olley steady Boy's head while he administered an antidote. Then, with a curt 'thank you' to the groom, he suggested they take it in turns to sit up all night, Jake to take first watch.

When Olley had gone to his quarters above the tack-room, Tamsin started to yawn. They had been up at five that morning, but she settled down on a bale of straw opposite Jake without saying anything. Golden Boy was sweating and trembling, but eventually the medicine seemed to take effect, and after a while he began to calm down.

Eventually Jake's eyes met hers. 'Are you going to tell me about it?' he demanded at last.

When she dropped her glance, he came across and crouched in front of her, gripping her by the shoulders so that she was forced to look into his face. Unable to bear such close contact, she struggled to get away, but he shook her roughly and rasped, 'All I want is for you to tell me what happened. I'm not going to turn you over to the police, Tamsin, but I must know.'

'Nothing happened,' she muttered, conscious of the sudden nearness of him and how her tiredness, his coldness and all the other events made her simply want to plead for his protection.

'He's giving you money, isn't he?'

He began to shake her, reading off the admission of guilt from her face like reading a page from a book. She began to cry.

When she didn't answer, he shook her again. 'Tell me the truth, will you?'

Suddenly something seemed to snap inside her and she shouted, 'Yes! He paid me! So what? I took his money and said I'd persuade you to sell Golden Boy.'

'He didn't get much for his money, did he?' For a moment his face lost its harshness, then a movement from Golden Boy in the straw brought it back. 'So you thought you'd try another angle? Lord, how could anyone stoop so low?'

She felt his grip tighten on her upper arms. 'You're hurting——' she muttered, pushing ineffectually against him.

'It's nothing to what I'd like to do.'

She raised a tear-smeared face. 'I didn't know he was going to try anything like this, Jake. I thought it was a simple question of talking you round—you can't say that's against the law. It seemed reasonable enough at the time. In Chantilly. But when I got here and—well, I decided not to go on with it. Let him have his money back.'

'Really?' It was obvious from his tone that he didn't believe her. 'Why the sudden about-face? Wasn't he paying you enough?'

'I just changed my mind,' she repeated stubbornly.

'You must have had a better reason than that.'

'I've told you the truth. Now, let me go!' He was too close for comfort. If she'd wanted, she could have counted his eyelashes.

'So,' he tried another tack, 'when did you send this "fee" back? Was it when you realised you'd never be able to do what he asked? That was honest of you.' He paused when she neither confirmed nor denied his theory. 'Well?' he prompted.

'That's not the whole story. It just came to seem wrong,' she went on, glossing over the fact that she hadn't actually sent Emile's five hundred back even now. To confess that would damn her for ever more. 'I hadn't properly thought it all out. And when I saw how much Golden Boy meant to you. And...' She let her words trail away, for how could she tell him that it was after meeting him that everything had changed for her? He'd think she was simply trying it on again. 'Oh, please, Jake—that's the whole story, really it is...'

He was obviously in two minds whether to believe her or not. 'If there's anything I don't know about, Tamsin, you'd better tell me while you've got the chance, or I'll...' The threat hung unspoken in the air. 'Listen,' he said quietly, 'I'm giving you the chance to clear yourself.'

She couldn't bring herself to add anything to what she'd already said. When she didn't answer, he said gently, 'He compromised you, is that it? And you, being you, haven't the humility to admit he made a fool of you.'

Suddenly reaching out, he took her face between his two hands and cradled it against his shoulder. 'You didn't know what to do, did you? How could you be a match for a snake like him? He'd make it seem like a simple errand. And you were unable to resist the reward he promised you. He played on your unhappiness...'

For a moment he held her against his chest, and she could feel the power and security of being wrapped in his arms. It was everything she wanted, and she responded by clinging tearfully around his neck as if she would never let him go.

'I've wanted to hold you in my arms for so long,' he murmured, 'but you've created so much suspicion. Even now, I could be putting the horses at risk——' He looked down at her tear-besmirched face.

'Believe me, please, Jake,' she whispered, burying her face in the side of his neck. 'I never guessed it would turn out like this. You do believe me, don't you?' You must, she thought frantically to herself, seeing a vestige of the doubt he wasn't trying to hide even now.

'It's a long way to come, only to change your mind the minute you get here,' he observed.

Not knowing quite how to convince him, she pressed her face against the side of his neck and clung to him with her arms around his neck. Soon she was kissing him, allowing her lips to explore the strong jawline, the hollows beneath the dominant cheekbones, tracing the little lines on either side of his mouth. When she reached the corners of his lips, she felt too shy to kiss him properly, and simply fluttered her lips lightly over his, retreating again and again until she became bolder and he began to groan with pleasure.

'Please believe me, Jake, darling,' she whispered, scarcely daring to say aloud the words of love she wanted to speak. Their two mouths played a game of hide and seek, first one, then the other, touching then retreating, teasing and tormenting each other, as if unwilling to go too far, yet unable to stop. He caught her hands and placed them underneath his thick sweater, where they discovered a life of their own, exploring the solid muscles, travelling inside his shirt, revelling in the texture of the hard male body beneath their touch.

Although he murmured encouragement, he made no attempt to kiss her more fully. She began to feel desperate for reassurance. 'Please, Jake, believe me. Say it, please, darling, please say it to me. Please say you believe me.' It was on the tip of her tongue to say she loved him, but modesty held her back at the last minute. Instead she let her lips linger more lovingly close to his, even now reluctant to be the first to dare so much.

He lay back, eyes closed, a half-smile on his lips. As she began to withdraw her hands, he caught them and put them back. 'Don't stop! I believe every word you utter. I just had to ask you, kitten. I had to be sure.'

Slowly he began to direct her hands to the buttons of his shirt. Her fingers slipped inside and caressed the warm flesh. She darted a small kiss in the gap of his open shirt. Then his hands groped through her loosened hair, pulling her head down closer still against his chest. Her lips began to move of their own accord, giving little bites and kisses all over his skin.

'Take your jacket off,' he suggested, moving to unfasten it as he spoke. 'Now mine.'

He guided her hands so that it slid down off his shoulders, then he pulled her down beside him in the thick, clean straw. He was already directing her hands to the fastener of her jeans when she hesitated and he reached up to turn off the overhead light.

A faint glimmer from the yard lamp filtered through to them. In its light she could just make out the lines of his face, the eyes hooded in shadow, their expression hidden. Golden Boy was breathing easily and regularly in the far corner of his stall.

With a shiver Tamsin felt the rough straw on her naked back as he pulled up her lambswool sweater, then she was sinking back into the straw as his weight moved down on her.

'Don't stop what you were doing before, kitten. It was wonderful,' he groaned as he discovered her soft breasts beneath his hands.

Tamsin was filled with alarm at what lay ahead. She had started kissing him out of a desperate attempt to convince him she wasn't as bad as he suspected, but now, once again, the water was deeper than expected. This was something she had secretly wanted all along, but it was also something for which she was not yet ready.

Jake sensed her misgivings. 'Cold?'

'It's not that.'

He wrested the initiative from her by allowing his fingers to slide inside her jodhpurs. It made her shudder with pleasure, but she clasped his wrists between both her hands, whispering, 'No, don't, Jake, please don't.'

'Don't tease me, kitten. We really need each other.' He buried his tongue in her mouth, and she began to move her head wildly from side to side as she tried to wriggle out from under him. Yet when he opened blurry eyes as if to release her, something, her own desire, fought to bring her aching body close again.

'Steady, angel,' he whispered.

'Jake, I can't,' she choked. 'I don't know how...' For a moment she felt his warm body lapping over her own, then he tensed as her words registered. For a long moment he held her in his arms.

'Tamsin?' His voice was hesitant. 'What are you saying?'

'You know what I mean,' she replied in a small voice. She felt his body shudder for a moment, bringing his desire under control with an effort. Then he pulled her up to sitting position, so that she was nestled in the protective crook of his arm.

'Tell me properly.'

'I'm sorry. You must hate me,' she muttered, burying her face against his shoulder. 'I'm sorry I'm so boring.'

His warm laughter made her peer through the shadows at the expression on his face. From out of the dark, his eyes seemed to flash with liquid light. 'Tamsin, Tamsin,' he murmured, repeating her name again and again as he moved his hands over her quivering flesh. 'Boring is the last word I'd use... But I'd rather you knew exactly what you were doing.' He began to stroke her gold hair, pulling out the separate curls as if they were the most wonderful things he had ever seen.

'I want you so much,' she whispered, astonished at her own boldness. As if to prove it, her body undulated against his, causing him to groan aloud.

'Stop it, kitten, or you'll make me lose control, and I don't imagine either of us want you pregnant just yet.' He deliberately held her at arm's length, and then with obvious regret began to drag her sweater back on over her head. 'Let's go up to the flat for a drink. It's time Olley came down to take over here. Come on. We'll be sensible and see how things turn out.'

She was in no doubt how they would turn out when his mouth claimed hers again and their bodies started to draw towards each other like magnets pulled by an inner force. Too overwhelmed by desire to think sensibly, she scuffed around in the dark for her coat. She would go anywhere with Jake, whatever the consequences. He made her feel like she'd never felt before.

'I'll have a quick look at Boy,' he told her. 'Switch the light on for me.'

A click of the switch filled the loose-box with a metallic glare. When their eyes got used to it they blinked at each other, as if seeing each other for the first time. Jake's eyes were luminous with desire.

He went over to the horse and ran an expert hand over its body, looked in its mouth, under its eyelids, then pronounced himself satisfied with his progress.

He was about to rejoin Tamsin by the door when he gave an exclamation and bent to pick something up from where it was half-hidden in the straw. Tamsin turned to look. Then she froze in horror.

There, in the palm of Jake's hand, was a crumpled white envelope. And, even as she lunged forward with a little cry to try to snatch it away from him, he was drawing from it an incriminating plastic bag containing two large horse pills.

Her hands rose to her face as if to blot out the sight, but nothing could shut out the exclamation of cold fury that now issued from Jake's throat.

He didn't need to ask what it was. Even without the typewritten letter which he now drew forth and started to read in a voice of deadly calm, she knew he could put only one interpretation on it.

Too dismayed to think straight, she swivelled and abruptly left the stable, stumbling blindly across the yard until she came to the field gate. Then she started walking. There was nothing ahead but the black of night, and behind her nothing but the silence of Jake's huge and justifiable fury.

CHAPTER SIX

INDIFFERENT to her fate, an owl on the hunt flapped eerily overhead. Somehow Tamsin had lost her way in the dark, and an unexpected wood lay like a tangle of menace ahead.

Wondering which way to go, she decided to try to find a way round it. The owl put her off, its wild screech presaging carnage to come. Just by turning her head she could see the stable block with its lights shining out over the countryside. Dark shapes crossed and recrossed the beam of light, giving the place an air of peopled intimacy. She yearned to be back there once more.

Setting off in what she hoped would eventually turn out to be the direction of Rose Mead, she hadn't gone far when she came out on to a mud track that dipped down between high hedges of thorn. After another five minutes it brought her out into a ploughed field. There, straight ahead, to her utter chagrin, were the stables again.

Her exclamation of dismay froze on the air. The dark shape of a horseman was slowly emerging from a thicket half-way down the field. He was coming straight towards her at a slow canter.

'Tamsin!' It was, of course, Jake. In her beige riding breeches she must stand out like a beacon against the black hedgerow, she realised.

'What's the idea? Do you realise you've been walking round in circles?' He brought the horse right up to her and, before she could think to escape, had slid off its bare back and grasped her by the sleeve as if to prevent her from running off.

'What are you going to do?' she stuttered, frozen to the spot by his air of cold fury.

'Do?'

'I can explain——' She knew it was useless. She started to shiver. 'It isn't what it looks like, Jake. Please. You've got to believe me.'

'Tell that to the police,' he grated. 'You've given me all the evidence I need to nail that snake. As his accomplice, you'll take the rap with him. You'll both get what you deserve——'

'But you can't—please! I swear I wasn't involved. Truly, Jake! You must believe me!'

He gave a scathing laugh. 'You're so convincing, Tamsin, sweetheart. If I hadn't got that letter, I believe you could convince me even now.' His fingers convulsed round her arm. 'Why do I fall for your lies whenever you widen those innocent green eyes at me?'

He dragged her close up against his hard body, and in the half-light she saw his eyes glittering over her face and his lips hovering so tantalisingly close that, despite his words, she thought he was going to bring them crushing ruthlessly down on to her own. At the last minute he drew back.

'You'll go to prison.' His lips twisted and his glance searched her face for every little change of expression.

There was a long silence in which she had time to note how pale he looked, his skin almost luminous in the moonlight, night shadows giving him a wild appearance.

'When you come out,' he ground on after a moment, 'you'll have lost everything you ever had—looks, name, friends—and any hope you might have had of making a career for yourself in show-jumping.'

Her teeth were chattering so much, she couldn't say anything.

'Didn't you bother to think of the consequences?' She dropped her glance and his grip tightened round her body, as if trying to force an answer out of her. 'Moral qualms aside, they should have been enough to make you think twice.' A nerve twitched at the side of his mouth. 'Or were you so deeply involved with de Monterrey that you'd do anything he asked of you?'

'No! Not that, Jake. Don't think that!'

'Don't waste your breath telling me it's not true. I'll never believe another word you say.'

'I'm not involved with Emile himself at all,' she protested.

'He must have had some hold over you. Don't try to deny it.'

'At least believe me when I say I'd never hurt you or Boy, or anybody deliberately. Whatever it looks like, you must believe that.' Her heart was breaking into a thousand fragments as they stood facing each other under the night sky. It was desolation outside and within. He seemed unmoved by her protestations. But they were standing so close, she could hear their two hearts beating in unison.

Then, before she knew what was happening, he was dragging her over to the place where his horse was cropping grass.

'Get up,' he ordered. He gave her a leg up, bundling her on to the back of the horse without any further explanation, then swung up behind her before flicking the lead rein to urge him on. Jake's arm was clasped around her waist, and she could feel his body pressing against her back, with the long length of his thighs matching her own in spine-tingling intimacy.

They rode like this towards the distant lights of Brantingham. Despite her fear of what lay ahead, Tamsin couldn't stop herself responding to the heaven of his touch, no matter that for him it had nothing to do with love. He ignited fires that wiped all else from her mind.

When they reached the stable yard, Olley came out from Boy's stall. 'I'll see to Bowman,' he said gruffly with a carefully neutral glance at Tamsin.

Jake hustled her along the lane to the house. When they got inside, he surprised her by saying, 'I'm shattered. Time enough to call the police in the morning.' He patted his pocket. 'All the evidence I need is here.'

He pushed her towards a flight of open-tread stairs that led up to a first-floor landing.

'You'll sleep in there.' A door swung back to reveal a neat, masculine room with horse prints on the walls and a bedside-table piled with riding magazines.

'What about you?' she hedged, noting the single bed and the evidence of use. Her knees were trembling uncontrollably.

'Don't worry about me.'

Her heart fell. Catching her expression, he gripped her suddenly by the chin. 'I wouldn't touch you now, Tamsin, if you were the last woman on earth. Not after that performance in the stables.' He gave a short laugh. 'If it's any consolation, I actually fell for what you said then. You were totally convincing.' Disgust at his own stupidity was evident in his whole manner. 'When I learned you'd been with de Monterrey for six months, it was ob-

vious you must have been lovers. I just didn't want
to believe it. I hoped you'd have better taste.'

His expression was bruised. Noting it, she
thought, maybe it's fatigue. Or maybe even now,
despite his words, he really feels something for me.
Please, Jake, she pleaded silently. Please trust me,
want me, love me. Then the words were wrung from
her.

'Jake,' she said, 'I think I love you.'

Once said, she knew they were the words that
had been crying out to be said for so long.

There was a stunned silence, then, pulling himself
together, Jake gave her a sardonic appraisal that
went on long enough to make her wish she'd held
her tongue. 'I'll give you one thing,' he said, 'you're
a trier.'

With that, he pushed her right inside the room,
closed the door, turned the key in the lock, and
then she heard his footsteps recede to another part
of the house.

Next morning her door was unlocked at eight
o'clock. She had lain awake all night and heard
him get up at six-thirty in the half-dark to see to
the horses. He had been back in the flat for half
an hour before he bothered to come up to let her
out. He was holding a bath towel. 'Have a shower.
Get dressed, then come downstairs.'

Resentful as she was at being ordered about, she
saw she was in no position to argue. White-faced
at the thought of the police cars that would be
coming to cart her off, she followed his instructions, presenting herself in the kitchen twenty
minutes later.

There was a breakfast of toast, eggs and black
coffee waiting for her.

'It's like the breakfast before a hanging,' she observed with a flash of her old spirit. A glint in the depths of the brown eyes showed that he had registered her mood. With her hair scraped back into a damp bunch behind her ears, she hadn't bothered with make-up. The amber sweater she had worn yesterday when they had set off for Badminton felt grubby and her jodhpurs were stained with hoof oil.

'You look a wreck,' he observed with satisfaction.

'It hardly matters, does it? You don't expect me to dress up for the police mug-shot, do you?'

His smile was quite genial, alerting her to further punishment.

'I'm not turning you in just yet. I've had a better idea. Sit down.'

Reluctant to obey this constant ordering about, she stood mutinously beside the table before she realised that he was going to tuck into his breakfast whether she stood or sat, so she plumped down in the straw-bottomed chair opposite and started to fiddle about with the piece of toast he pushed towards her.

'Cereal?' he asked, pouring himself a liberal helping straight from the box.

'For goodness' sake,' she muttered edgily, 'can't you get straight to the point? Get me handed over. Let's get on with it.'

'Getting through to you, is it?'

'Yes!' she snarled. 'Satisfied?'

'Hardly.' He paused. 'But I aim to be, one way or another.' He paused again and took a sip of hot black coffee. Tamsin restrained her impulse to scream at this deliberate ploy to keep her waiting. Eventually he said, 'Let's just go over what you told me last night.'

'Must we? I'm not going to change my story. It was the truth. I've nothing more to say.' She jutted her chin and tried not to show how frightened she was under the brash exterior.

'You still say you changed your mind on a whim after having said yes and accepting payment from de Monterrey?'

'I didn't put it quite like that, did I? It makes me sound like an idiot.' His silence and his smile drew a snarl from her. 'Just dial 999 and get it over with!'

'I told you, I've got a better idea.' He leaned back, a spoon of cornflakes half-way to his lips.

'You're enjoying playing cat and mouse, you rat!'

He laughed aloud. 'I want to be sure I'm being fair. Though why I should give a spoilt brat like you the benefit of the doubt——' He broke off when he noticed her look of relief. 'Don't think you're getting away with it. Not after what you've done. But I want to nail him once and for all, and you're going to be the one to help me. It's a condition of your release.'

She blinked. 'Help? How?'

'I'll go into details later. But first you're going to get in touch with him. Let him think you've done as he asked. Then you're going to demand a bigger slice of the cake.' He gave a bitter smile. 'I'm not having Golden Boy undervalued. You can tell de Monterrey I'm still being difficult to persuade—which, of course, I am.'

'Damned difficult,' she agreed ironically.

'Well, I don't wish to be accused of making you perjure yourself,' he added, matching her tone.

He leaned back confidently on two legs of his chair. 'You don't need to know anything else. All you have to do is do as you're told.'

This last remark stung her, as no doubt it was intended to. 'And if I don't?'

In answer he merely drew the fingers of one hand across his throat.

'What else are you going to make me do?'

'You'll see.'

She shuddered. 'What's to stop me warning Emile what you're up to? I mean, isn't that what you'd expect—given that you're convinced I'm in league with him?'

'Don't worry. I've already thought of that, and as there's no way I shall ever trust you again,' he told her matter-of-factly, 'what I'm going to do is make sure you can't contact him—or anyone else,' he added with an ominous smile.

Tamsin's mouth went dry. 'You can't do that.'

'Why not?'

'Well——' She searched frantically for anything that would stop Jake Newman doing exactly what he wanted. 'You'd have to keep me a prisoner, or something like that——'

'Precisely.'

She gaped at him. 'You can't.'

'Why not?'

'Where could you——? I mean—whereabouts——?'

'Here.'

A look of disbelief sketched itself over her face. 'Your people will be pleased when they find out.' She glanced round the cosy little kitchen. Outside the window, the L-shape of the main house lay just across the courtyard.

'You forgot, they flew to Madrid yesterday, for three weeks,' he said, following her glance. 'And there's no one else nearby. Saul won't miss you.'

He glanced at his watch. 'He'll already have touched down at Dublin airport by now.'

With a sick feeling, she suddenly saw that he was right. Nobody from the stables would help her, especially if they heard from Jake what she was supposed to have done. There was no one. Helplessly, her eyes strayed to the phone on the wall. He laughed softly.

'Will you try to ring him? Please do. Be my guest. That would be the same as a confession of guilt. It'd be all I needed.'

'I hate you, Jake!' She turned to glare at him.

'That's more like the truth.'

Last night's blurting of her love for him swam into her mind with embarrassing clarity. She blushed. 'Oh, you think you're so clever, Mr Newman!'

She bit back the rest of the insults that were piling up waiting to be uttered, and with an effort tried to match his cool manner by leaning back in her chair and regarding him for a moment with a slight smile on her face. 'I shall contact Emile only if and when you tell me to. If that's what you need to prove I'm innocent, that's what you'll get. You're going to have to eat your words, Jake.'

'Naturally, I haven't counted out the possibility that you're far too clever to betray yourself,' he warned her with a slight smile. 'If you've any sense, of course you won't let me catch you getting in touch with him.'

'Don't you sometimes feel you're too clever for your own good?'

'Cut it out, Tamsin. I don't have time to sit here bandying words with you. To make sure you're kept busy while we await developments from the other side of the Channel, you're going to train with me every day.' He gave a grim smile. 'Let's see how this much-vaunted ambition of yours stands up to reality. By the time I've finished with you, you won't want to see another horse in your life. I'm calling your bluff, kitten. That's what. I'm going to give you what you say you want—a hundred times over.'

He finished off his breakfast and piled his dirty crockery into the dishwasher. 'Hurry up. We've got a lot to do.'

The first thing they did was go over to Rose Mead to pick up some clothes.

'Nothing fancy,' he told her curtly. 'You're not going anywhere special.'

Stonily she ripped a few jumpers and skirts from their hangers and tossed them into the suitcase she had brought back from France. 'You're stark, staring mad, Jake,' she accused. 'What's to stop me just walking out?'

'You won't, unless you're definitely in it with Emile. And why should I care? I've still got the letter.'

She registered this, acknowledged it to be true, and filed it away to be pondered over later. 'You must have some personal vendetta against him to go to these lengths.'

'Do you think he should be allowed to get away with what he's done, just because this time he happens to have failed? Surely you don't imagine it's the first time he's tried to pull this particular trick? I've heard a lot of stories since I put the word out that I was interested. And I don't care for what I've heard.'

'Where's the white charger?'

He suddenly loomed over her. 'Don't get funny.'

Something in his manner sent a spiral of fear up her body. Now he was standing over her, so close, so menacing, she was unable to block out the horrid fact that she was completely in his power. Yet despite his air of menace her senses picked up the animal magnetism he exuded. It scattered her thoughts wide and far, sending a look of helpless sensuality into her eyes which he registered at once.

He pulled her roughly to her feet, and their bodies touched briefly before he stepped back.

'You've got enough clothes for now.' He picked up her suitcase, pushing her in front of him and following her out. He didn't glance at her once on the short drive back to the estate, but she saw how tense he was, how white his knuckles were on the steering-wheel. It was as if his whole demeanour emphasised how much he despised her.

'And now we'll see whether you can get horses over jumps as you claim.' Jake had had one of the novices saddled up. He was black, big and full of oats, side-stepping and tossing his head and giving little bucks as he was led out into the school. When he saw the jumps, he started to show the whites of his eyes and to back up against the kick-board, the drumming of his hooves audible even in the yard outside.

Jake was watching Tamsin's face closely, and she wondered if he was looking for signs of reluctance—anybody would be cautious about getting too close to such a violent-looking animal.

'What's his name?' she asked.

'Satan,' replied Jake casually.

She took the reins and got a nip from Satan as she did so. It was going to be no good trying to pet this one like a kitten. 'He's built well,' she observed, forgetting her own problems for a moment. 'What's his history?'

'Think he's got one?'

'He's remembering something nasty,' she remarked. 'Look at the way he's backing off from those jumps.' Jake was still watching her. She didn't care now. If he thought he was about to call her bluff, as he put it, he had another think coming. If she could make him respect her a little, then, maybe, with a little more luck, he would begin to thaw towards her. Then he would realise she was telling the truth, and after that, perhaps he would once again take her in his arms...

'I think I'll walk him round for a while.' She pulled herself together, forcing herself to pay attention to Satan and almost missing Jake's complacent nod. He thinks I'm too scared to get up, she thought as she began to walk the horse firmly round the ring.

For the next few minutes she was scarcely aware of the watchful figure in the gallery. All her attention was on the challenge Jake had thrown down.

Little by little, Satan began to trust her. She showed him the jumps, letting him have a good sniff at them, patting and talking to him all the while, then when he wasn't prepared to resist she slipped neatly into the saddle.

As she had expected, he wanted to dislodge her. His hindquarters swung round and his back legs started to work like pistons. Calmly driving him forwards, she made him trot round the ring until he was used to her weight, then when he was quiet she urged him into a slow canter. He was still spooking at everything, but he had settled into a sort of grumpy acceptance of her control. And every time she rode past Jake she felt his eyes fixed in concentrated attention upon her.

Satan had such a big stride, he seemed to cover the length of the school in three bounds. She knew he would be a great jumper, if only he could conquer his fear. The first jump she presented him at was a low brush fence. She could have jumped it herself. But Satan came roaring towards it then jammed on the brakes, all four legs stuck straight out.

The momentum carried her half-way up his neck. At once he began to sweat and tremble. Regretting her haste in forcing him to the jump, she turned him away and trotted towards the gallery.

Tossing her whip up to Jake, she called. 'Maybe that's what's bothering him. If he's still panicky next time around, I'm going to leave it for now.' She didn't care if Jake thought she was giving in. It wasn't fair on Satan. There was a genuine fear in him, and she didn't intend to beat him over the jumps just to please Jake Newman. With a little time and patience he would begin to show his true form. Then, she was sure, he would be magnificent. Lucky Jake, she thought, turning her back and setting to work once more.

Jake was still sitting up in the gallery when she eventually persuaded Satan over a double pole lying flat on the ground. Even then the big horse began to sweat and tremble. 'That's enough, old fellow, there, there,' she murmured as she slid to the ground and went round to fondle the animal's head.

Jake appeared silently over the deep saw-dust of the ring. 'Hardly competition standard,' he observed caustically.

'Me or the horse?'

'Oh, we all know you're the star of the pony club,' he came back.

Knowing that he was trying to bait her, Tamsin couldn't help holding her breath as he approached. His black hair fell over his brow, but the cold, chiselled features didn't warm towards her. In fact, he seemed strangely agitated and almost snatched Satan's reins from her hands.

'Are you going to show me how it's really done?' she asked.

He gave her a silent look. 'Let's have some lunch.'

In the days that followed, the pattern of that first day was repeated. They rose at six, after spending the night in their separate rooms—Tamsin's, after that first night, thankfully unlocked. Then the morning was taken up with routine chores in the stables, afternoons being reserved for work with whichever of the horses Jake told her to ride.

Usually by nightfall she was so dog-tired that she wouldn't have wanted to go out even if he'd suggested it, so it was a relief to find that he expected her to curl up with a paperback or watch television. He was often on the phone. She heard him turn down several invitations.

'You don't have to do that on my account,' she told him once, looking up from the book she was reading.

'I'm not, don't worry,' he replied coldly, switching on the nine o'clock news and becoming immediately engrossed.

'It's quite like being married,' she gibed later as she brought him a mug of cocoa before turning in early.

He looked up from the depths of the armchair, his amber eyes glittering through narrowed lids. 'Don't get any ideas.'

The truth was, despite her outward calm, Tamsin was feeling the effects of being cloistered with him morning, noon and night—so close, yet as distant as if they were living on separate planets. She longed for a touch, a smile, a sign that he still desired her— that, if nothing, would have made her imprisonment bearable. But he seemed to have switched off all feelings for her, and, when she lay night after night in the cold single bed, she cried with longing for him.

She began to wish that Emile would get on with his rotten scheme, but it was taking time for her letter, dictated by Jake that first morning, to go through the post, and she guessed it would also take time for Emile to weigh up the pros and cons before getting in touch with her again.

On the fourth or fifth morning, Tamsin went along to Jake's bedroom as soon as she woke up. It was still dark outside. A wafer of moon hung in the gap between the curtains.

'Jake!' she called softly. He was a silent mound in the bed, but sat up as soon as she called.

'What time is it?'

'It isn't time yet. Listen, I can't go on like this. You're tearing me apart——' The darkness made her bold.

'I'm doing no such thing. Let's not have any melodrama, Tamsin,' came the clipped tones from across the room.

'I can't sleep,' she went on. Her voice began to waver, but she forced herself to continue. 'I think I'm sickening for something. It's probably psychosomatic. I'm never ill. But I feel terrible. I can't concentrate. I'm starting to do stupid things like putting toast in my coffee.' It was all true. Even he must have noticed the change in her. 'I'm going to do something dangerous soon—and I won't be able to help it.'

'Is this some sort of threat?' he asked from the bed.

'Of course not!' She shook her head, even though he probably couldn't see. Her long reddish hair was still tousled from where she had been tossing and turning on it all night long, but she was making it worse now by continually teasing out the curls that trailed to her shoulders.

'Come here.'

She moved a little closer in her bare feet and he reached out to trap her hands, 'Stop doing that. It's becoming a nervous habit. I've noticed that much.'

'I feel as if I'm sitting on a powder keg,' she burst out. 'I thought this was all going to turn out to be some sort of sick joke. I've told you I'm sorry and I've tried to explain how I got involved, but you won't believe me. You're going to force me to go through with it to the bitter end. Jake...' She bit her bottom lip. 'I can't go on.' The warmth from his sleep-filled body was sweeping towards her, overpowering her with waves of cogent desire.

'You have to go on. You have no choice. You should have thought of the consequences before you got involved with him.'

'You won't believe I'm not involved with him in that way,' she stated tonelessly. It was useless. She had nothing left to argue with. She turned as if to leave.

He reached out with one hand and felt for her in the dark, pulling her down against the side of the bed when he managed to grasp hold of her. 'I'm curious to see how far your loyalty to your lover will stretch. So far it's quite impressive.'

She couldn't tell whether he was being sarcastic or not. How did he expect her to behave?

'He's not my lover. He never was,' she muttered. 'Why won't anything I say convince you? What can I do?'

Jake was caressing her face with one forefinger. It was a consoling, hypnotic movement, but there was an intent expression on his face. His dark eyes seemed to glitter in pools of shadow. She felt him move so that his face hovered close to her own.

With a feeling of 'what will be will be', she let him take her in his arms. There was no point in fighting him. He controlled everything. And he could turn her on as easily as turning a key.

Waves of desire surged over her as he began to loosen the ribbons of her nightgown. The soft cotton rippled over her skin as he pulled it to one side.

'Breaking point?' he whispered.

'Yes... Yes.' She turned her head to hide the blush that stained her cheeks.

He pulled her down on to the bed so that she was lying half under him, and his hand came up to part the tousled locks covering her face. She kept her eyes shut, surprised to hear herself give a little moan as his hands continued their exploration inside the slit of her nightdress. He found her breasts and began to stroke them gently, his movements becoming suddenly wilder as he felt her nipples harden against his palm. Then his lips sank into hers at the same time as their tongues met, probed, fought, then circled, melting. In a moment she could scarcely tell whose mouth was whose— flesh seemed to meld into flesh, and wherever their bodies touched was one pulsing flow of feeling.

She heard herself cry his name aloud as her lips twisted to take his weight. Now it didn't seem to matter that she didn't know what to do, for his body released from hers all its innate knowledge, and a primitive instinct took over, sending her messages that responded directly to the movements of his body. His breathing was harsh, hardening proof of his own desire, enticing a response as blind emotion took control.

She cried aloud all the unfamiliar words of love that were being wrung from her depths as she felt his movements begin to release her into womanhood. Again she moaned as an instant's pain gave way to a conflagration so intense that it sent her body writhing like flame, as if fires burned the fringe of heaven. She was soaring now in realms of joy, as if there was no way back from these newly discovered pleasure lands, unable to believe such ecstasy could ever end, clutching at the broad, bronzed back, the muscles rippling under her fingers as he pleasured her again and again until she was melting, floating, dissolving in the ecstasy of the moment. A million stars seemed to burst overhead as a unisoned cry brought them spiralling earthwards.

Tears started to cascade down her cheeks. She gasped his name again and again, as if finding hidden meaning in it. Shudders of satiety were running through her, and at first only her rippling fingers teasing over the athlete's shoulders centred her. Then her lips began to brush his skin, fingers ruffled through the coal-black hair, and she became still within his embrace, and a languor overtook her, drawing her down into a formless world of dreams.

When she awoke in his arms a little later he was looking at her through eyes that seemed blurred. It was lighter now, as day broke. A grey light, in which his eyes were like dark lakes where she could drown herself. She shuddered again in the aftermath of surrender, but before she could move he rolled over to one side, hearing her cry out with the sudden loss of his touch.

She saw him glance down at the crumpled blue sheet that lay between them. After a long pause she was pulled to the surface again by his clipped tones.

'Fairly inconclusive, alas.' His voice snapped her eyes open.

'What is?'

He gave her a strange, derisive look.

She felt cold when he moved away and tried to snuggle back against him, hooking herself somehow underneath his bent arm so that he had no choice but to lie half on top of her. Then she began to pet him with little kisses and nibbles to make him stop looking so stern and remote. But he shook his head irritably, rolling abruptly on to his back, and pulling up the dark blue duvet, to gaze moodily at the ceiling without explaining.

Greatly daring, she ran her fingers down his body like a piano player, but he moved away again and a sudden freeze cracked through her.

'Jake?' She raised herself on one elbow and tried to get him to look at her.

He averted his face. 'More?' he asked bluntly. His eyes were bruised-looking, making her heart turn over.

'I don't understand. Are you angry?' She knew it shouldn't be like this afterwards. 'Did I do something wrong?' How could it be wrong, when it had been so wonderful?

'I wish you had done something wrong. Unfortunately, your performance was most professional.' He turned his head so that the dark eyes were looking straight into hers.

She bit her lip. 'I don't understand,' she repeated.

'I guessed you'd give yourself away in bed, but I didn't want to risk finding out the truth. It should be obvious what I'm saying. And don't waste time giving me that "little girl lost" look.'

'I'm not giving you any sort of look,' she told him with candour.

'Little innocent?' His mouth twisted.

'Not now——' She tried to smile, but her lips had stiffened and wouldn't function properly.

His own lips compressed in an unforgiving smile.

'Everything you've ever told me has been lies, nothing but lies,' he intoned. 'I must have been crazy to fall——' He broke off, scowling. 'I wanted to be fair to you, to believe in you. When you told me you had a purely mercenary relationship with de Monterrey, if that wasn't bad enough, at least I tried to believe you...but there was obviously more than that between you. It's been plain all along. I shut my eyes to it. Despite the stories.'

'What stories?'

His mouth twisted. 'You must have heard the ones about de Monterrey's stud farm.'

'But he hasn't got a stud farm yet.'

'Precisely. But it's common knowledge he beds all his stable-girls——' His voice was savage.

'That's just a malicious joke,' she broke in.

'One he takes care not to counter.'

'Look, I don't care what they say. I'm not one of his girlfriends. I've told you over and over again.' She raised herself on to one elbow. 'He made certain promises about—about things,' she haltingly explained, reluctant to tell him about the threatened smear of her father's name while he was in this suspicious, unforgiving mood. 'All I had to do was persuade you to sell Golden Boy.'

'And your reward?'

'He would help me get back into show-jumping,' she mumbled, turning scarlet at the half-truth.

'No strings?' He gave a hard laugh. 'And you expect me to believe that? You also said you were a virgin, remember? "I don't know what to do," you told me in that sweet little innocent voice.'

'Well?' she flared.

Suddenly he threw the duvet back and sprang from the bed. 'Get out!' His face was grey. The expression in his eyes shrivelled any words she could utter in self-defence, and she cringed back. Yet even in the midst of her own anguish she longed to reach out her arms to him, to comfort him.

Dragging herself up, she pulled on her nightdress with shaking fingers. 'How can we move from that——' her eyes went to the tumbled bed '—to this?' She raised her stricken face to his. For a moment their eyes locked.

Deliberately he said, 'If you want "that" again, let me know.'

He turned to the door, cutting off her cry, and dragging on a scarlet robe to conceal his beloved body from her gaze.

'Jake!' she cried, willing him to turn back. A knot of emotion rose to strangle the rest of what she longed to say. She heard him switch on the shower, turning it up full, drowning out her presence. It was as if his every action condemned her to the emptiness of rejection.

CHAPTER SEVEN

TAMSIN'S body felt like an open wound. If she had felt pain before her early-morning visit to Jake's room, now she felt ten times worse. Everything hurt, from the sight of his dark face, averted from hers, to the intimate pitch of his voice excluding her from his idle banter with the staff. Even the accidental touch of his hand as they both reached for a piece of tack at the same time seemed to sear her flesh. And the familiar scent of lime and leather, as he leaned close in order to hold Satan's head while she bent to adjust the stirrup leathers, choked her with the memories it brought back.

As they worked side by side throughout the days that followed, she could have put a brave face on the fact that he didn't seem to see her any more, if only she could have believed it would all come to an end soon. But it was obvious he had written her out of his life for good.

As soon as he had enough evidence against Emile it would be goodbye forever.

For the first time in her life she took refuge in an attempt to please. All her chores were done as quickly and faultlessly as she knew how.

It was six-thirty. The end of another long day.

Jake was draped against the wooden saddle-horse in the tack-room. He had been watching her for some minutes. 'Tired?' Directed straight at her, the question made her jump, the yawn prompting the remark covered half guiltily by one hand. 'I told you it was tough.' He was unsympathetic.

'I can cope.' She ignored the derisive glint in his eyes and placed her coffee-cup on the wooden tray with the others so that whoever was on washing-up roster could take them through.

Jake called to Lin in the next room. 'Don't forget to drop by Rose Mead to pick up Tamsin's mail, will you?'

She came through, ready to go, and patted one, of her pockets with a smile. 'I've got the key.'

After she went off, Tamsin gave him a cold glance. 'There was no need to send her. I can pick it up myself later. Except there won't be any mail.'

'So you might have me believe.' He returned her glance, frost palpable. 'I'm busy this evening and haven't time to escort you over there.' His distrust was being ladled out in buckets full. She felt sick.

There was no time to dwell on the chill this incident shed, for she was kept busy, settling the horses for the night. By the time all the preparations for an early start next morning had been made, it was already dark.

They made their way back to the empty house in a silence that was becoming habitual. It seemed desolate with the main part of the house now unoccupied. Jake's adjoining barn conversion looked bleak, too, as they went inside.

He moved about, switching on lights, turning up the heaters, pulling the curtains across, while Tamsin set about preparing an evening meal. She clung still to a pathetic desire to please, and embarked on a complicated recipe with ingredients raided from the freezer. She was just reaching into the back of a cupboard for the blender when Jake noticed what she was doing.

'I don't want anything elaborate at this time of night. An omelette will do. And I'll make it.'

'But——'

'Please, Tamsin.' He looked bored at the prospect of an argument. But Tamsin was driven by concern.

'You look as if you need a good, square meal. And with the show tomorrow——'

'For heaven's sake! Is this what marriage would be like? Thank heaven I've opted out. Open a packet of soup if you want to justify your existence.'

Without a word, she replaced all the stuff in the freezer and went to the dried food cupboard. He must live on packet soup, she thought, staring at the jammed shelves. It was the first time she'd heard he'd opted out of marriage altogether. She had thought it was only a question of who did the chasing.

'Tomato, country chicken, asparagus, mushroom——' she began to reel off, but he stopped her impatiently.

'Your choice. I chose the second course.'

Very fair, she thought, not daring to say it aloud. She chose the one she thought he would choose himself, then absent-mindedly managed to let it burn as she cut some slices of bread for the toast.

'Brilliant,' he remarked as he sniffed the air. 'Luckily, I never did like oxtail. Put the pan on the draining-board with some bleach in it, and have a shot at cream of vegetable.'

'You should have told me,' she muttered.

'What?'

'That you didn't like oxtail.'

'And have you burn the one I really like?'

'It wasn't deliberate,' she retorted irritably.

'No? Never heard of the subconscious? You're a walking ball of fury. You know you can't get back at me, so you take it out on the soup.'

'Poor, defenceless soup. I didn't realise you were a shrink in your spare time. I suppose the elaborate meal I was planning was done to get at you as well?'

'Quite probably.'

'I would have thought it more likely to be the other way round,' she replied tartly.

He raised his eyebrows. 'I've no reason to be angry with you. You're hardly worth it. Sympathy would be more appropriate, considering the mess you've got yourself into. You know you can only go on hurting yourself. And it must be impossible to accept that I've stepped in and snatched the reward you were looking forward to from out of your grasp.'

She bit back the retort that sprang to her lips and became thoughtful. 'I hadn't looked at it like that,' she said, trying to analyse her reactions. 'But I would only feel angry if I thought I'd been in the right to begin with. As it is, I now know I was a stupid fool. I can see you feel justified in keeping me in this open prison until Emile walks into your trap...'

She hesitated, and he broke in roughly with, 'So you agree I'm right?'

'I suppose so.' She bent her head. 'It's just——'

'Yes?'

'It's just—I feel despair more than anger now. I know you're wrong to suspect me. You're wrong, Jake.' She twisted a tea-cloth in her hands. 'It's despair. Not anger.'

'Spare me.' He turned his back. 'You never give up.'

He broke half a dozen eggs rapidly into a bowl, whisked them, poured the mixture into a flat-bottomed pan, and turned out an omelette a few minutes later with the aplomb of a man used to fending for himself.

Tamsin watched, thinking, he doesn't need anybody. Such self-sufficiency, though it shut her out, attracted her even more.

She brought the soup to the table and managed to rescue the toast just as it started to go black round the edges. They had to eat the omelette at the same time as the soup.

'You're a domestic disaster,' he observed with satisfaction. 'Heaven help your husband, should you manage to catch one. I suppose you always had a cook?'

She nodded, avoiding his glance. 'At least I can usually produce a passable cup of coffee and mix a martini.'

'We'll test that boast later.'

'Do you need to? You should know by now that I never claim to be able to do something if I can't.' To her surprise, he didn't come back with some sarcastic gibe as she had half expected. It was as if he accepted she'd scored a point.

It must be to do with the way I've handled Satan, she thought. The horse had really taken to her. Today he had jumped a wall, a small one, but he had gone over like a lamb. Lin told her afterwards that it was the first time she had seen him jump anything.

'How long have you had Satan?' she asked.

Jake's head jerked up. 'That's a *non sequitur*, isn't it?'

'I didn't think it was.' For a moment they eyed each other levelly across the table. Then Jake threw back his head and began to laugh. Tamsin's heart lurched with desire.

'OK, clever,' he said, not unkindly. 'You've worked a miracle with him. I picked him up at the sales at Wetherby a few weeks ago because I liked the look of him. Trouble is, he hates men. Wouldn't let me near him for three weeks, let alone take him over jumps. Then you walk in and have him eating out of your hand in five minutes.' He grinned. 'Pity your talents don't extend to the rest of the male population.'

'I don't usually have problems,' she retorted. Then her eye caught his, pulling the corners of her mouth upwards in a sudden answering smile. For a moment there was a truce, then, as if he regretted it, he pushed his empty plate to one side and stood up. Before she could stop him, he thrust the dirty crockery into the dishwasher and started to fill the percolator with water.

'Coffee?' he asked gruffly.

'I said I could make it.' She was desperate to make amends for the 'crime' he was holding against her. But he didn't answer, instead turning on the kitchen radio and adjusting it so that it was just too loud for the intimate level of conversation towards which they had been sliding with such nerve-fraying ease.

The rest of the evening was spent in what to any outsider would have seemed like a kind of domestic bliss. Jake sat at the desk in the corner of the sitting-room, going through some figures, while Tamsin curled up in one of his big squashy armchairs with a book.

Every now and then she would look up to let her eyes trail lovingly over the dark head within the pool of light shed by the brass lamp on the desk

beside him. But never once did he return her glance.
He seemed capable of totally switching off from
whatever was going on around him.

By ten o'clock Tamsin was ready for sleep. The
narrow, cold, empty bed awaiting her was not in-
viting. When she told him she was going up, he
barely lifted his head.

Contrary to what she had expected, her eyes
closed as soon as her head hit the pillow.

Struggling to focus next morning, the first thing
she saw was one of the striped mugs from the
kitchen on her bedside-table. It hadn't been there
last night when she'd fallen asleep. Sitting up, she
saw it was full of cocoa. Cold now. With a skin on
top. She felt confused.

Why he had brought it up seemed less important
than that he'd done so. She felt touched, scared of
putting a foot wrong as she got ready and went
down to greet him, pondering over what the day
might hold in store.

Jake was apparently still asleep when she went
down, and the kitchen was deserted. To make it
cosy, she switched on the light. It was still half-
dark outside. Then she tuned the radio to a cheerful
music programme and began to busy herself with
breakfast. It was a labour of love, she knew, grilling
rashers of bacon with sausages, tomatoes and eggs,
and preparing everything to a split second, just the
way he liked it. The toast, golden and crisp, popped
out of the toaster as if on cue just as he came in.

If he was surprised at the cosy domestic scene
that met his gaze, he showed no sign. As soon as
he sat down, she whisked the food on to warmed
plates and set it in front of him. The coffee was
excellent, piping hot and black, and there was lots
of it. She pushed his favourite cup towards him.

'Thanks,' he muttered briefly. When she hung about, wondering if there was anything else she could do for him, he asked, 'Aren't you eating?'

'I've had some toast.' She'd had to dispose of her first attempt somewhere.

'That all?'

'It's all I want.'

'It's going to be a long day.' He didn't pursue the matter.

To please him, she poured herself another cup of black coffee. He was watching the clock. When it got to half-past he pushed back his chair. Without giving her more than a passing glance, he suggested they make a start.

He wore a preoccupied expression and, thinking he was worried about the day's forthcoming classes, she did her best to make sure everything was ready. All his kit was laid out. The pink jacket, the white breeches, the clean white shirt, the stock, his boots polished to a glowing lustre. She had double-checked everything, even though she knew he had prepared everything himself the night before.

She fetched his jacket now, keeping it on its hanger for the journey down, and tucked the rest of his things neatly into his holdall. The boots she tucked under one arm, then turned to him. 'Ready.'

Their eyes met accidentally, but the expression in his was ambiguous.

'Really?' he asked, with a roughening of his voice.

She nodded, trying to ignore the message that flashed automatically between them, but she couldn't hide the telltale colour that mounted instantly to her cheeks.

He gave a sardonic smile. 'Let's go.'

The air outside was sharp and fresh. Dawn was tinting the paddock with rose and gold. A thousand fragments of light splintered and glowed as they waded through the long grass in the lane. Tamsin breathed in the crystal air with a shudder of pleasure. It was all so beautiful here. Jake strode ahead, oblivious to everything. A lump formed in her throat.

For a moment she was tempted to run beside him, to remind him how they had greeted another dawn. It must mean something, she cried inwardly. But, fearing another bleak look from those dark eyes, she walked slowly on behind him and held her tongue. He would be irritated by a break in his concentration just now, and she had to do all she could to show him she wasn't like all those other women, the husband-hunters, the ones only interested in adding a famous name to their lists. She smiled bleakly at the thought of lists.

Olley was sitting in a cloud of cigarette smoke in the cab of the horse-box when they arrived, and the horses were all on board. Lin was having a gossip with a couple of the other girls while she waited, and everyone turned to stare as Jake and Tamsin appeared through the early-morning mist from the direction of the house.

Tamsin blushed at the thoughts going through their heads when they saw her trailing along behind Jake. Pity would be uppermost. Lin had jokingly warned her that he was a heart-breaker. To them it must be an old, old story.

Half-way down the motorway, they pulled into a service station. Tamsin followed the three of them into the garish green and yellow cafeteria. Olley nipped into the gents, and while Lin went on ahead to get a table Tamsin followed Jake past a row of telephones under smoked perspex bubbles into the queue. The sight of them made something suddenly come to mind. He was holding open the swing doors for her, but she hesitated before passing through.

'You must know I'm not going to try to ring Emile. You must!' she said.

He followed her into the queue.

'If I've given up helping him, I won't need to ring him. Assuming I was helping him in the first place.'

'Which you were.'

'Yes, but——' She was confused. 'I'm not, Jake.'

'Stop doing that,' he ordered in a bored voice.

'What?' She felt tired all of a sudden.

He brought a hand up and took hold of both of hers with a suddenness that made her gasp. 'It's a nervous habit. Stop it.' He pushed the strand of hair she'd been fiddling with back behind her ears. 'If you're on the level, there's no need for all this. It's just a question of sitting it out.'

Automatically her hand went up to her hair again.

'Stop it, will you? Or I'll get them to plait it up like Satan's.' For a moment his eyes softened, then the same bleak look returned.

'Trust me, please, Jake. I can't bear for things to be like this between us.' She had never had to plead for anything in her life before.

'It's a waiting game,' he told her. 'You'll have to accept it.'

'It's all right for you—you have nerves of steel. What if he doesn't do as you expect? How long do we go on like this?'

'Does it matter? You're doing the job you want. We're having fun.'

'Fun?'

'I told you to let me know when you wanted—more.'

She turned blindly to the display cabinet and chose something at random. Her hands were shaking as she placed something wrapped in plastic on the tray.

Little knots of autograph hunters stood around the ground all day despite the drizzle and a sharp, biting wind. Tamsin noticed without surprise that the largest group were fans of Jake's. It wasn't surprising—unlike some of the other riders, he didn't look diminished the minute he dismounted. He was the most handsome man in the place.

Today he was riding with a remote expression on his face. Even in the excitement of the jump-off his mask didn't slip. He managed to clip so many seconds off the record time, it was scarcely worth the other riders going back in. She saw him flex his shoulders as he waited in the competitors' enclosure as the results came through.

When he went up to receive the big silver challenge trophy, amid an exceptionally warm response from the crowd, the flashing of the Press bulbs marking his path, his face still looked like an iron mask.

'Well done, Jake,' said Olley. 'A good omen for the big one.' He took charge of Chelsea, and Jake thanked him, turning to Tamsin as she stood watching.

'Come on, I need a drink.' He barged through the autograph hunters without his usual genial signing, and pushed her towards an empty stretch of white rail overlooking the dressage arena.

'I thought you wanted a drink,' she remarked.

'In a minute.'

'I'll go and get you one, if you like.' She knew what it would be like in the wine tent. He was obviously tired now the main event was over, and wouldn't relish being the focus of attention.

'What's got into you? Is it a belated attempt to prove you'd be good wife material? Just stop fussing, will you? Or,' he paused, 'perhaps you've seen someone you want to have a word with in there?' He indicated the marquee behind them.

'If there had been anyone I wanted to have a word with, don't you think I'd have done it while you were out there in the ring?' She paused for a moment. 'As it is, I haven't been able to tear my eyes away from you all day.' She blushed as she spoke. Unused to such feelings, and too shy to feel happy about being so blatant, it was his indifference that forced her to speak her mind.

His response was predictable. 'Same old approach. Same old reason, no doubt.'

'Don't, Jake. Don't shut me out.' She took a deep breath. 'Before we go back to the crowd, there's something I want to ask.'

'What?' He looked bored and allowed his glance to stray to the ring as if anything she could say would be of far less importance than what was going on there.

'I want to know what you thought happened between us——' She hesitated, finding such frankness difficult.

'When?' He raised his eyebrows as if he couldn't imagine the answer.

'The other morning. In bed,' she spelled out, unable to stop herself from blushing, and angry when he didn't pretend not to notice.

'I would have thought,' he replied slowly, and with a cold half-smile on his lips, 'that what happened was obvious to the greenest *ingénue*—which you——' he paused significantly '—most certainly are not.'

Her sudden intake of breath went unheeded. The smile still played around his lips.

Words Saul had once said came rushing back. Jake, he had told her, was a man who liked to see for himself. Could he then have devised a test in cold blood—a test which involved taking her to bed? And now she had somehow failed it, was he seriously using it as an excuse not to believe anything she said? Was that it?

Something in her refused to believe he could stoop so low, but his expression was as unrelenting as ever.

'You're wrong. Not that you'll listen.' The wobble in her voice was audible. 'What else can I say?'

'Words shouldn't be necessary.' He turned his head away. 'Can we stop this? Your life's your own. Who you've been to bed with, or indeed how many men involved, are questions for your conscience alone. The only possible concern to me is that it's just one more lie to add to all the rest.' Still without looking at her, he went on, 'You've shown how ambitious you are, and it's obvious you have a great deal of talent as a rider. But you've let your ambition get the better of your integrity.'

Tears sprang into her eyes at his sheer stubbornness, but she blinked them back. 'That's so damned unfair, Jake. It's so unfair!' She felt like screaming the truth at him to force him to believe her, but, knowing it was no good, she swallowed her anger down.

He took her silence to mean she had nothing more to say. 'The irony is that you had no need to get caught up in anything like this. If you'd written to me from France, I would have given you a fair trial. Heavens, your name would have been enough to give you a foot in the door. If you'd shown up well, as of course you would, I would have signed you up like a shot. It's all been so needless.'

He gazed out across the arena. 'Anybody would have taken you on. It'll be difficult now, when this gets out. If it does.' He turned to peer down into her upturned face. 'Oh, Tamsin, you're good. There's no doubt about that. So what stopped you going about things properly?'

Tamsin's mind flew back to last winter when her homesickness had been so strong, but her fear of returning to England as a total failure warred against her natural inclination to come back; and she remembered Emile's threat to rake up all the old scandal again, making it impossible ever to return. And she thought also of her beloved father, and the unfairness of people, because he had thought more of life than money.

'It seemed too difficult,' she told him lamely. 'I can't explain——'

He turned to look at her now, the brown eyes sharp, layers of unexpressed emotion deep within them. She could tell he was disappointed. He knew she was holding something back. But he went on, 'And what about this other story? How are you going to talk your way out of that?'

Her eyes widened. She wasn't sure what he meant, but he enlightened her by saying, 'If you'd been honest and not told me such a lie about still being a virgin—for heaven's sake——' He broke off.

'I don't expect girls to be totally inexperienced at your age. How old are you?'

He peered closer, suddenly noticing the tears flowing silently down her cheeks. He put out a finger and let them fall on to it without speaking for a moment, then he said, 'What are these for? Has it finally hit you that you've lost the opportunity of a lifetime?'

'To ride for you?' She shook her head, angry with herself for showing how vulnerable she was. When he pulled out a handkerchief and tried to dab at her tears, she shied away with a little cry of protest.

'You don't realise what happened, do you?' She backed away from the handkerchief and his efforts to wipe her tears with it. 'You still don't know!'

With a sob she turned and started to run towards the shelter of the marquee. Her anger was as much for the casual way her virginity had been thrown away as for her inability to make him see that she was telling him the truth.

'Tamsin! Come back!'

A glance over her shoulder showed that he was about to come after her. She turned and fled into the side entrance of the marquee, nearly tripping over the guy ropes as he came charging after her. Inside, there would be sufficient number of people to make him think twice about getting into an open argument.

Before she could lose herself in the crush, he came up behind her, slipping an arm around her waist, effectively preventing her from getting away without drawing attention to herself. She turned to him with a careful smile for the benefit of anyone watching, and said in a quiet voice, 'I'm getting out of here. Don't stop me, Jake.'

'Why shouldn't I stop you if I don't want you to go?' he murmured, pulling her up close against him, despite the fact that they were becoming the focus of attention.

'I'll cause a scene,' she warned, with another false smile for the benefit of their audience.

Jake mirrored it. 'And if you start a scene, my angel, I shall have no qualms about finishing it— to your embarrassment rather than my own.'

They eyed each other like two fencers, waiting to see who would make the next move.

'I suppose even scandal is good publicity for a fame-hound like you,' she gibed. He was too close for comfort, and she tried without success to edge away.

'I'd have the further advantage that everyone would be on my side. It can't have escaped your notice that as far as this lot are concerned I can do no wrong today.'

'Don't let it go to your head.'

'Whereas for you,' he went on, ignoring her interruption, 'it wouldn't be the same at all. In fact, it might be some time before you dare show your face in public. The newspaper boys would eat you alive.'

She began to tremble violently at how close he skirted to the truth. Bracing herself, she said as lightly as she could, 'Perhaps I could sell my story and make a fortune?'

'Let's hope it wouldn't be as disastrous as the last attempt.' His mask slipped and the dark eyes shone wickedly.

'Don't touch me like that, Jake.' The hand wrapped around her waist was beginning to move up and down her spine underneath her jacket, unseen by anyone. It was the most erotic thing she could imagine. She tried to control the surge of desire rising with such frightening rapidity inside her as the unmistakable meaning of that bright look hit her.

'Still hyped up after your win?' she managed to drawl, trying to distance him. 'You show-jumpers are more like rock stars every day. You're insatiable.'

'You can hardly say that, angel. I've been living like a monk ever since you came on the scene.'

'Don't let me change the scenario. Feel free to carry on as usual—with your fans,' she added hastily, in case he took it as an invitation. Suddenly his presence was everywhere. She felt enveloped by it. The milling crowd seemed to recede. His eyes were stripping her and touching her, whipping her desires to a state of trembling suspense. Her bones were melting under his touch and her legs trembled, scarcely able to support her. She put out a hand, gripping his lapel to steady herself.

'I've never seen anyone look so aroused by a mere touch before.' His lips scarcely moved. 'If I could only get rid of Olley and Lin, I'd take you back to the van right now.'

'Don't tease, Jake,' she breathed, confused by the force of her reaction.

'I've never been more serious in my life. You do things to my judgement that nobody else can manage. When I saw you watching me in the ring today, I nearly ordered the judges to have you removed.'

He pulled out a strand of the red-gold hair, twisting it sensuously between two fingers. It was an act of flagrant eroticism, and sent a shudder of desire coursing through her again. Some instinct suggested that if she told him the truth right now he would definitely believe her, despite himself.

'Jake, about the other time. It was really the first time for me. I didn't know it was like that. Now will you let me go? Please?'

He gave a start, as if suffering a body blow. His face acquired a stunned expression, and while he was coming to terms with what she had just told him she managed to slip quickly through a gap in the crowd and make her escape outside.

The afternoon was drawing to a close, and the stall-holders all along the makeshift street were beginning to pack up their wares. Tamsin slipped behind a parked van full of animal feed and headed for the tea tent. It was the one place Jake would not be likely to follow for fear of being mobbed the minute he set foot inside.

A steaming mug of strong tea helped to bring her pulses near to normal. She sat on a wooden bench, unnoticed by the crowd, and thought about Jake. She wondered if all girls felt so dizzy when the man they had fallen for flirted so outrageously with them in a public place. She'd somehow missed the teenage years, and felt out of her depth with Jake's no-holds-barred flirting, despite the air of sophisticated glamour she could adopt when the need arose.

Emerging from the tea tent a quarter of an hour later, she wended her way towards the competitors' enclosure, reaching the horse-box just as Jake himself sauntered up.

'Thought you'd been kidnapped. Where have you been?'

'Ringing Emile, of course,' she replied flippantly.

A hand shot out and gripped the wrist she brought up to defend herself. The glint in his eyes told her clearly to watch her step. He released her with a small smile, but there was something ambiguous about the expression on his face. 'Get in the van. We're going home.'

There was just room for the four of them on the front bench. After the episode in the marquee, Tamsin wondered how she would survive the long journey ahead, with Jake's muscular body pressing insinuatingly against her own. She could feel the muscles of his thigh jammed against hers as Olley bumped the horse-box over the rough grass towards the road.

Her senses were beginning to dizzy when, with the same ambiguous expression on his face, Jake leaned close and pushed something into her hand that brought her spinning back to the present with a sickening thud. It was a Press photograph of herself and Emile on the night he had taken her to dinner. Emile had his arm around her, possessiveness etched into every line on his face. The caption in French hinted at a soon-to-be-announced engagement.

'You're full of surprises, aren't you, Tamsin?' he began pleasantly. 'Just an employer, eh? And why on earth didn't you tell us he also goes by the name of Jerzy Moreno?'

CHAPTER EIGHT

CAUGHT off-guard, Tamsin could only stare back at him in astonishment. 'Jerzy who?' she eventually managed to ask.

'You heard.' Jake leaned across to Olley, raising his voice above the roar of the engine, 'That was the name, wasn't it?'

Olley gave a gruff assent.

'We've been finding out a lot about your friend,' Jake went on. 'The old man gave me some interesting snippets on his career the other evening, confirmed, I might add, by Saul, and——'

'So that's why you were so offhand with me when we went to Badminton? But Saul would have told me if there was anything I should have known——' She broke off.

'Perhaps he thought you knew? I didn't get time to go into it with him.'

Tamsin bit her lip and gazed stonily out of the window. 'It's true I don't know much about Emile... There were rumours, of course. Anybody's who's had instant rise to fame and fortune can expect mud-slinging.' She gave Jake a pointed glance. 'I've always thought it rather unfair to believe all the stories that happen to circulate.'

'Why? Don't they say, where there's smoke——?'

'You would say that... Just because you're lucky enough to get on well with the Press.'

'I have nothing to hide.'

111

'Neither had my father, but they made a meal of his affairs after he died.'

'And Emile?'

'Has he anything to hide?'

Jake's face lost all expression when he heard her talk as if she were defending him. 'Loyalty is one of your strong points, is it?'

'He wasn't very likeable, Jake,' she tried to explain. 'People delighted in gossiping about him.'

'But you liked him.' His lip curled.

'No.' She paused. How to describe the mixture of fear and pity she felt? She didn't want to go into all this, anyway, not with Lin and Olley present, and maybe not even without them. 'He was a different era from me,' she went on lamely. 'Men of his age, forty or so, they're often still living in the Dark Age as far as women are concerned. It's unpleasant, but it's no excuse for trying to—oh, I don't know!'

She rubbed the back of her hand across her forehead.

'I'll tell you what we've found out,' he went on. 'As the name Moreno seems such a surprise to you, it may interest you to know that he isn't Count anything—he's no more a Frenchman than I am. He picked up his phoney title ten years ago for a few thousand French francs.'

'Really?' Her tone was scathing.

'A few million, then. I don't know what the going rate is these days,' he said, deliberately misunderstanding her.

'What nationality do you think he really is?' cut in Olley, to stop what seemed likely to develop into a private wrangle.

'That's not really the issue,' observed Jake impatiently. He turned to Tamsin. 'You suggested I had some personal vendetta against him. Well, in a way I have. So, probably, have quite a lot of other people who can't stomach his business methods. He's been on the verge of being thrown out of French racing for some time now, but he's always managed to talk his way out of it. However,' he looked grim, 'he's made the mistake of extending his sphere of operations elsewhere.'

The three of them were watching her as Jake explained. He gave a wry smile. 'He had the bad judgement, Tamsin, to fix a couple of Olley's brother-in-law's horses——'

'Sorry?' Tamsin was lost.

'My brother-in-law's a jockey,' explained Olley. 'Young lad. Up and coming. Least he was, till the finger of suspicion fell on him.'

'Suspicion?' Tamsin looked from one to the other.

'Two of the horses he was contracted to ride suddenly lost form. He was dragged before the jockey club. They thought he'd had a hand in it himself.' Olley looked disgusted.

Jake continued the story. 'Both times a mysterious foreign buyer stepped in and picked them up for a song. And they both finished up in stables at Chantilly where they went on to make their new owner a splendid profit.' He gave her a sardonic glance. 'Like it?'

'This new owner...?'

'You've guessed it.'

'Emile.'

The shock of it showed clearly on her face. Noticing, Jake hesitated for a moment, then he added, 'The scene in France was getting too hot for him, so he turned his attentions to the British show-jumping circuit. And you were the instrument.'

'The man's nothing but a horse-trader.' Olley was disgusted.

'I can't believe it,' Tamsin said simply. But she did. And her expression must have shown clearly enough that she believed it, too.

When they arrived back at Brantingham Hall, she went straight over to the flat as soon as all the chores of bedding down the horses were done. Once inside, she made for the kitchen and put the kettle on.

Stretching and yawning, Jake stood in the doorway, looking in at her with a bemused, slightly quizzical expression that she didn't understand. She turned her back. He looked unbearably attractive. With his tousled black hair just asking to have her fingers run through it, he looked almost cuddly. He looks sweet and gorgeous, she thought, but in reality he's as dangerous as a panther.

'This is a domestic little scene,' he observed as he watched her take two mugs down from the cupboard and begin to wrestle with the lid of the cocoa tin. Suddenly he was by her side. 'Let me.' He reached out and took the tin from her fingers, prising off the lid and handing it back with the same odd smile playing round his lips. She had to force herself not to tremble at his nearness.

'This is still a novelty,' he went on. 'A female coping with my bedtime cocoa.'

'Don't your girlfriends make themselves useful?' she asked pointedly.

'Yes, but not in a domestic sense,' he quipped.

Determined to keep the mood neutral, she merely smiled, pretending that the cocoa-making required her full concentration. Wanting him so badly frightened her. But his revelations about Emile had confused her, too. She didn't know what to think.

It had confirmed something she had managed to shut out of her mind until now. But it still wasn't something she wanted to dwell on. Emile was a snake. She'd always known that. And he had blatantly used her to try to swindle Jake. His innocent hankering to own Golden Boy had been a blind for something much bigger. She felt like an utter fool. Yet a more pressing problem was Jake—and what was going to happen next.

'You didn't have any idea about Emile, did you?' he ventured as she began to pour the boiling water into two striped mugs.

'How could I? I was only a stable-hand. I only know what he told me.'

'You're a gullible little fool,' he murmured, coming up close behind her and wrapping his arms around her so suddenly that she was trapped against the side of the kitchen units.

Without daring to turn her head, she asked, 'Why are you doing this, Jake?'

'Can I ever make amends, kitten?'

Too late, she half turned and the lips nibbling her ear slid over her own as if they were coming home. When she thought she would probably faint with desire, he lifted her hair from the nape of her neck and began to blaze a trail of fire over her skin, stopping just below the tip of her ear, into which he whispered, 'Since you ask, sweet, I'm doing this because I intend to take you to bed...but first there's something I must know.'

He toyed with the thick hair in its black velvet ribbon, pulling on the bow at her nape until it snaked free and her hair cascaded in all its glorious abundance to her shoulders.

He seemed reluctant to pose the question, but with a strong movement that brought her curving back against his body ran his hands over her flat stomach and down to her thighs before bringing them back to caress her breasts. He buried his face in the luxuriant hair. Then, as if fearing to hear her reply, he asked rapidly, 'Did you really never let him make love to you?'

Tamsin broke free with a little gasp. 'Of course not.' She bit her lip before confessing, 'It is true, Jake, he did ask me to become his mistress. It was the night the photo was taken.'

'Tell me about it.' He pulled her round so that she was facing him. She began to tremble as she felt the full length of his hard body matching her own line for line with breath-stopping intimacy. He locked her in his arms with her head tilted back as if to make every nuance of her expression visible.

'It was a sort of formality with him, to ask that,' she told him. 'And when he learned I was no longer the heiress he thought I was, he was only too glad to get out of any further entanglement.' The memory of Emile's sarcasm when he'd learned she was the same as all the other girls who worked for him and still dared to turn him down still rankled. He had found it hard to believe that the shock-waves of financial disaster caused by her father's unexpected death had reached out to engulf her, too. He could hardly credit she had been left without a penny in the world.

'He knew your father?'

'Knew of. Who didn't?'

'And that's why he thought you had money?'

'I suppose so.' She lifted her head. 'A lot of people regarded me in a different light when they learned I'd become a pauper.'

'So now you have to prove yourself?'

'What's wrong with that?' She tried to push him away.

'I haven't finished yet.' He tightened his pressure so that she was effectively trapped.

'Finished what?' she demanded hotly, avoiding his glance. 'This inquisition?'

'Yes,' he smiled faintly, 'if you want to put it like that. I'd rather see it as an attempt to find out what makes you tick.'

'Is it worth it?' She glared at him. She was no longer sure whether it was particularly erotic standing like this with him if he was going to scold her like an uncle.

Then he started to stroke her hair. 'I think it's probably worth it. On balance.'

'There's nothing else to say anyway, so you're wasting your time.'

'Did you ever sleep with him?'

Her lips tightened. After her confession earlier, when she'd had to screw up her courage even to mention the subject, he had the gall to ask her that again!

Too furious to answer, she let the silence lengthen until he broke it by asking in a surprisingly quiet voice, 'Are you still feeling hurt because he ditched you as soon as he found out about your circumstances?'

'Hurt?' There seemed to be miles of misunderstandings between them. She didn't know how to begin to explain. She would have pushed him out of arm's reach if he hadn't looked at her again with those dark, deep, all-seeing eyes, the expression of sympathy and forgiveness in them too much to resist. It's a trick of the light, she thought wildly; he only looks as if he cares. It's probably just curiosity. She'd been the victim of that before today.

But his calm attention began to pull the words from out of the hidden depths where they had been long buried, and she found herself blurting out the whole story.

'I'd always expected him to make a move, ever since he'd offered me a job out of the blue.' She gave Jake a cool glance, not easy with his body pressed almost abstractedly against her own, making her senses flare to the point where it was difficult to concentrate.

'The thing was, he never made any definite sort of move until I'd been working for him for about six months. By then, of course, I was off my guard.'

She tried to ease away from Jake's weight, but he shifted with her and they settled into an even more comfortable position, his arms criss-crossed behind her back, holding her close.

With an effort, she brought her mind back to what she was telling him. 'Eventually, when the fateful meeting came, it was a relief to be let off the hook so easily, and what he was asking seemed so innocent—come here, persuade you to sell a horse, collect my commission and a little bit of help with my career. What could be more straightforward?'

She grimaced. 'I must have been blind not to see what his game was. He took me to one of the top restaurants that evening, and I have to admit it was heaven to wear lovely clothes again, to feel the heads turn as we walked in, to feel special again.'

'Is that how he persuaded you to do his dirty work for him?' Jake looked incredulous.

'Not quite.' Her eyes became pools of darker green. 'There was something else.' Jake was watching her with such quiet intensity, she could hear his heart thudding. 'He said, "If you want your former life of luxury, as I suspect you do, I can help you''. Naturally, I listened.'

'Didn't you feel suspicious?'

Jake was rubbing the back of her neck with his magic touch, and Tamsin tried hard to concentrate. 'A bit,' she admitted, 'but the way he put it made the result inevitable. He said, "You have two choices. Either you do this simple task for me, for which I will pay handsomely, or——" Then he paused.'

Jake's fingers tensed. She could feel the change of pressure underneath her hair. 'Or what?' he prompted.

'"Or I will tell the world that your father was a swindler and a thief." He told me he had letters to prove it.'

Jake relaxed, but his frown deepened. 'Did you ask to see them?'

She opened her eyes wide. 'I must have been totally freaked by his air of menace—I didn't even ask!' She gave a shiver. 'I must have been mad. But you must remember, Jake, he's quite a powerful figure over there. If money equals power, then he has power. I just felt I had to make him keep quiet at all costs. And it seemed such a little thing to ask me to do.'

'What did you say to him?' asked Jake more briskly.

'I had no idea how I was going to go about it once I was here, and to be honest I didn't give it much thought. I was just so determined I wasn't going to let him drag Dad's name through the mud again that I jumped at anything to prevent it. Even so,' she continued, 'I told him at first that I couldn't do it.' Her eyes were storm-green. 'He said, "My dear, have you a choice?" I said that I didn't have to do anything I didn't want to. If things became unpleasant there, I would hand in my notice. He asked, did I imagine I would "necessarily find it easy to obtain employment elsewhere in France?"'

'That was a direct threat to get you talked out of employment.'

'I know it was. And I was just about to tell him where he got off,' her eyes glittered, 'when he started to talk about you, and Boy, and the old days when, in Saul's words I used to be "the poppet of the Royal Enclosure"—and I have to hand it to Emile, he really knows how to play on one's weaknesses. Suddenly I began to see it as a challenge. Had I got what it took to pull it off? I guess gambling runs in the family!'

She looked rather shamefaced, but any thought of not being totally honest with Jake was out. 'Of course, he kept coming back to father's reputation. That was the clincher. I just couldn't bear the thought of anything coming out that I couldn't clearly disprove. And if Emile had letters, even if they were forgeries, as I knew they must be, it just seemed too risky...I know now I should have taken professional advice, but I thought I could handle it.' She lifted her head so she could look fully into Jake's eyes. 'I'm not proud of myself, Jake. I was utterly stupid. I've deserved everything that's happened.'

'Everything?' he murmured huskily.

She thrilled as his male body told her what he meant, and as it began to throb against her own she could scarcely take in what he was saying next. Then his lips came down to take hers, and her cry of surprise was stifled, turning at once into a moan of instantly awakened desire. His kiss, deepening, sent all other thoughts flying into oblivion.

'Jake, Jake,' she whispered as his lips sought other places on which to bestow their magic, the mere utterance of his name expressing all that was raging through her soul as his kisses flowed over her skin.

Her fingers began to rake through his hair, dragging his head down so that his probing tongue could fully explore the moist cavern of her mouth. They were both shaking with urgent need, and she was scarcely aware that he had picked her up and begun to carry her into the next room. Impatient hands were tearing at her clothes, and she twisted and turned in order to free herself from them while at the same time pulling at the buttons of his shirt, to speed the moment when his naked body would fuse with hers.

'I want you so much, Jake.' It made her feel vulnerable to confess it, but she had to admit what was in her heart. 'I want you more than anything else in the whole world.'

'More than anything?' A hint of derision showed briefly as he looked down at her.

She clung to him as his weight crushed down on her, dragging him tightly against her in a fever to have the ache of desire taken away. It was her answer to him and his mouth muffled her cries of pleasure as he took her completely, transporting her willingly into the wide oceans of delight.

He allowed her to guide him as she wanted so as to feed her own pleasure, hardly controlling his own needs until he felt the beacon of shared ecstasy beckoning them both. Then he took control, prolonging her pleasure until she approached the limit, carrying her with him to the edge until their cries joined together and he brought them both back to earth at last, Tamsin trembling in wonder as she clung to his damp shoulders.

'Where are we?' she asked some time later, opening eyes to the darkness surrounding them.

'In the sitting-room.' He laughed at her. 'I hope you can remember something.'

'Every second,' she told him with feeling.

He lay half across her with his cheek against her breasts. They were sprawled on the white goatskin rug in front of the fire.

'Shouldn't we go upstairs?' she asked.

'You're going nowhere, kitten. This is heaven enough.' He pulled up the soft wool rug so that it cocooned them both and, giving a contented sigh, Tamsin snuggled up against him. She was asleep within minutes.

When she woke up it was to see the sunlight streaming in through the loosely drawn curtains. A sigh of contentment escaped her as she remembered the heavenly hours of the night with Jake, her body feeling the unfamiliar effect of his possession, of possession by any man. She turned sleepily on to her side and then, with a little shock of surprise, sat up and looked round as her unfamiliar surroundings swung into focus.

There was evidence of their passionate haste the night before in the clothing strewn where it had fallen. And there was a hollow beside her, already cool. Jake must have got up to see the horses without trying to wake her.

Stretching like a contented cat, she rose from the tangle of rugs and cushions, pulling on Jake's black sweater as she went into the kitchen to fix a drink.

A glance at the clock told her that it was nearly eleven. Mildly shocked that she should have slept so long, she went up to have a shower, then pulled

on a turquoise silk shirt with a clean pair of tight-
fitting light-coloured trousers. Then, slipping into
her leather cowboy boots, she made her way out
of the flat towards the stables with a smile of expectation on her face.

Ahead lay an idyllic prospect consisting of nights
of glorious lovemaking, and days of working
alongside the most handsome man in England!
Another smile curved her lips as she dared to dream
of a future when there would be children, with
ponies in the meadow.

Melting in a lethargy of love, she hastened into
the stableyard, avid for a first glimpse of Jake's
broad shoulders, his handsome head, his smile, his
dark, devilish eyes, with today the evidence of a
shared secret within them.

The yard was empty. One or two horses poked
their heads inquisitively over their doors at the
sound of her footsteps. She hurried on across the
yard towards the school, pushing the wooden door
wide and running lightly up the steps into the
gallery, and then she stopped.

There was a visitor sitting up there. A stranger.
It was a woman Tamsin had never seen before. And
Jake, astride Golden Boy, was reined in beneath
the place she sat. Even as Tamsin approached, he
stood up in the stirrups and reached up to hand his
jacket to her. To Tamsin, watching unseen from
the doorway, it seemed as if there was something
possessive about the way the woman folded it and
placed it on her lap.

As she stepped through the door, Jake turned
back into the ring. He must have caught sight of
her out of the corner of his eyes, but instead of the
warm greeting she had been looking forward to he

merely raised the handle of his whip before driving Boy back on to the track.

Tamsin joined the woman on the spectators' bench.

'Hi, honey!' the woman greeted her warmly. 'I'm Mary-Lou. And you are——?'

'Tamsin Harland,' she replied, wondering what business of hers it was, as well as feeling mildly put-out that the stranger should take it on herself to make the introductions. Almost as if she had some proprietary right, thought Tamsin.

Unperturbed by her reserve, Mary-Lou stuck out a friendly hand. Long and slender, her fingers were loaded with gold rings. Heavy bangles chimed as she moved her arms. She had a deep, true tan, and, unlike Bianca the photographer, who had been making a play for Jake not so long ago, her blonde hair, worn in a sleek bob, was a natural-looking platinum. To Tamsin's chagrin, everything about her looked natural too, from her tan to her wide, white smile.

'That darling man! He's been putting his latest star through its paces for me.' Following her glance, Tamsin noticed Satan standing contentedly in a corner of the school. So Jake had been taking advantage of Satan's growing docility, had he? Trying to impress this newcomer?

'He manage all right?'

'You have to ask? On a monster like that, too!' Mary-Lou chuckled. 'He's poetry in motion.'

Tamsin didn't ask whether she meant Jake or Satan, but instead curiosity prompted her to ask, 'Do you ride?' She couldn't help the way the way her eyes picked out any evidence to the contrary— the frivolous high-heeled sandals, the pretty flowered two-piece. She needn't hope to get too far with Jake if she didn't ride, she was thinking. But to her surprise Mary-Lou laughed with evident delight.

'Why, I could ride before I could walk,' she drawled. 'I'm not your typical Southern Belle, no, sir—ask that darling man down there. Hey, Jakey!' she shouted with what seemed to Tamsin surprising strength and a marked lack of respect for Jake's dignity. 'Did you hear this? Tamsin asks can I ride horseback!'

Jake raised his whip, but carried on working Golden Boy round the school.

'How long you been around, honey?'

'Long enough,' replied Tamsin non-committally.

'You one of the regular staff?' Evidently unable to place her, Mary-Lou's glance flickered over Tamsin's unworkmanlike get-up, but Tamsin was saved from the bother of thinking up a reply because Jake was putting Boy at the wall and she could lean forward in pretended interest, as if she hadn't seen him do that self-same thing every day for the last week.

'Me, I'm an old, old friend of Jakey's,' Mary-Lou continued chattily. 'I guess I know him about as well as a woman can know a man, know what I mean? We toured the States earlier this year, and boy, do you get to know a guy's failings under those conditions?'

'You mean you were there when he was doing the American show-jumping circuit?' asked Tamsin, sitting bolt upright.

'Sure thing. It was a great experience. He's a real star over there, and rightly so.'

Tamsin was strongly tempted to say she thought groupies came younger, but bit back the words and tried to force a smile on to her slowly freezing features. 'Have you just come over?' she asked instead.

'Sure. Touched down at four this morning. Not as planned. I got chance of a flight earlier than expected. It sure was one hell of a shock for poor old Jake—he was expecting me tomorrow afternoon! Still, I saved him that drive down to Heathrow. He was sure glad enough about that, I reckon!'

Her glance fondly tracked Jake around the ring.

After her initial freeze, Tamsin began to burn with a sense of outrage. Despite her painful bout of honesty last night, and its sequel, Jake had himself been concealing from her an involvement of his own. No wonder he had been living like a monk, with the prospect of Mary-Lou turning up any day!

She felt humiliated. Then, remembering last night again, she began to feel a little sorry for the blonde American, after all. For surely she had presumed too much on her tour with Jake? It couldn't have meant much to him, otherwise he would never have been able to show such passion as he had last night, loving her as if she were the only woman in the world.

In a moment he would ride up and introduce her properly and Mary-Lou would be put in the picture, and somehow everything would sort itself out.

A few minutes later Jake did ride up. He looked straight up at her. But instead of the expected introduction he said, 'Late this morning.' He seemed preoccupied. 'Aren't you coming down?'

'Now?' She hesitated.

'Better late than never,' he remarked. His face was in shadow beneath the peak of the black velvet cap. 'I want you to take over here for me.'

Eager to show that she had a special role in Jake's life, she grabbed a hard hat and hurried down into the ring. As she walked towards Jake through the sawdust, he slid down from the saddle and led Golden Boy towards her, dropping the reins into her hands as he passed. She expected some greeting, a touch, a kiss even, but at the moment they drew level Mary-Lou called out, Boy jerked his head, and by the time Tamsin caught his reins Jake had gone on towards the exit.

She gazed after him in silent astonishment.

So she was the stable-hand once more, was she? At once all her previous suspicions came rampaging back. She glared as Mary-Lou gave a cheerful wave and sauntered down to meet Jake.

She decided she had better put her anger on ice for a while. At lunchtime she would find out just what Jake's game was—and his explanation had better be good!

'Lunch ready yet?'

Lin and Sue looked up as Tamsin's glance swept the tack-room as she came marching in. Finding no sign of either Jake or Mary-Lou she was momentarily put off her stride. Recovering, she went through into the kitchen and slammed about, putting the kettle on. No doubt Jake was still showing her around, trying to impress with his stable full of prize horses.

'Been playing you up, has he?' asked Lin sympathetically when she joined Tamsin in the kitchen.

It took her a minute to realise she meant Boy, not Jake. 'No, he's OK.' She began to butter some bread. 'Who's having soup?'

'Me, you and Susie,' Lin replied.

'What about Jake and—and his friend?' Tamsin held her breath.

'Mary-Lou you mean? Oh, he's taken her off to lunch at Halsham. Lucky devils!' She caught Tamsin's eye. 'I didn't know she was going to just turn up like this, did you? He might have warned us. I've been lumbered with Chelsea this afternoon, and I was hoping to go into Market Appleby to do some shopping.'

'No,' said Tamsin, 'I didn't know.'

Lin took another knife and started to help butter more bread for them all. After a minute she said quietly, 'Are you all right?'

'Yes.' Her voice sounded muffled. Lin noticed at once.

'Listen, I did try to warn you.'

'Warn me?'

'Everybody falls for him. It's an occupational hazard, working here.'

Tamsin stared glumly at the butter-dish. Then she raised her head. 'You as well?'

Lin shrugged. 'It didn't get far. But I made a real fool of myself, blurting it out one day. He was sweet. I guess he could have taken advantage.' She bit her lip. 'I hoped he would!' She sighed. 'It makes a change—stable staff are usually considered fair game. Trouble is, it made me fancy him all the more! He's a bloody decent chap, Tamsin.' She shot her a swift glance. 'Try to understand him.'

'Oh, I understand all right,' she replied with bitterness. 'But to be fair, he's never led me to believe there's any future at all.' With a shock, she realised this was true. Despite the heaven of being so intimate, he had never actually promised anything. 'Oh, hell!' Two tears as big as diamonds suddenly dropped into the slice of bread she was buttering.

'Brace up, Tam. It's not the end of the world.' Lin shook her gently by the shoulder. 'He's a heart-breaker; he can't help it.'

Tamsin dashed away her tears with the back of one hand. 'Yes, I suppose you've seen all this before.'

'He'll always have some woman mad enough to throw herself at him. I've watched them come and I've watched them go. But with you it's been different. He made a real play for you. And that's something I've never seen him do before.'

'What do you mean, *play*?' She remembered only his aloofness, the suspicions, the teasing and then, before last night, the apparent indifference again.

'His eyes never leave you. Haven't you noticed?' Lin smiled. 'You've been making us all as jealous as hell these last couple of weeks.'

'Well, look at me now!'

Later, when Jake and Mary-Lou had still failed to return from Halsham—from the restaurant Tamsin had somehow begun to think of as 'their' restaurant—tears soaked her pillow as she lay on her bed that afternoon. She had come straight back to the flat after lingering as long as she dared at the stables, and was waiting now for the sound of his car in the drive.

Not quite knowing what to do with herself, she got up and trailed about the flat. The sitting-room was still a mess, and she stood in the doorway, taunting herself with the memory of how it had got that way.

She had just made up her mind to fix herself a cup of coffee when the phone shrilled. Expecting to be asked to take a message for Jake, she nearly dropped the receiver when she heard the voice at the other end.

'Emile!'

'*Ma chérie*, Tamsin,' purred the familiar tones. '*C'est toi?*'

He broke into a flood of French. The reason for his call was obvious. The letter had arrived, and he wanted to know if she was alone so they could talk.

'I am alone,' she told him, 'But listen, Emile, I——'

'Darling, how is it going? Your letter was most clear. Of course I shall send you a further instalment. Just make sure you come up with the goods, yes?'

'Emile——' She stopped. This was what Jake had been waiting for. But he hadn't warned her how to handle the situation. She was confused.

'How is he, by the way?'

'Jake?'

'No, the horse.' He sounded slightly miffed by her misunderstanding.

In French, she explained. 'Apart from the fact that you nearly killed him, he's fine. Jake gave him something to pull him round.'

'What do you mean? He didn't suspect anything, did he?'

'Of course he suspected. He's not completely stupid, you know.' She was just sorting out the rest of her reply when there was a sound behind her.

Jerking round, she was in time to see Jake move from his position in the doorway where he had evidently been listening for some minutes, to judge by the mask of fury on his face.

Emile's voice came sharply down the phone, and while Jake shushed Mary-Lou, who was coming in noisily behind him from the car, she had to continue the conversation without being put off by what she knew was running riot in Jake's imagination.

Luckily Emile seemed satisfied with what she had said so far, even though things hadn't gone exactly according to plan. 'I will ring again in a day or two. You must administer the medicine, my dear girl. I shall expect a positive response next time we speak.'

He rang off, not, however, before Jake had come to stand next to Tamsin so that he could listen in to the endearments with which Emile concluded his call.

If anything, his frown deepened.

Tamsin turned a white face up to his. 'He rang me,' she told him before he could get a word in.

'Coincidence, is it not?' His voice was toneless with disbelief. He glanced towards the door. 'Mary-Lou, I'm sorry, this may take a minute or two. How about going across to the house? I'll join you shortly.'

'Don't be long, honey.' With a friendly wave she went out, closing the door behind her.

'He rang me, honey,' Tamsin said with as much scorn as she could muster.

'As I said, what a coincidence.' Jake's face seemed haggard.

'Coincidence nothing. He's probably been ringing for days, but we're never here.'

'So the first time you're here by yourself, hey presto!' Jake's voice was so toneless, it seemed as if he scarcely had the interest to speak to her. 'Surely you could come up with something more convincing than that? Your earlier attempt was convincing enough.'

'It was all true!'

'Really? Incriminating letters which the loyal daughter must conceal at all costs?'

'Yes. That's what happened——'

'It sounded far-fetched at the time. And now, this so aptly timed phone call. Come on, Tamsin, you know as well as I do, you're in it up to your neck.'

'Please, Jake, I'm really telling the truth.'

'Yes, yes. Just like before. You built up a house of cards. One lie revealed and the whole show comes crashing down.' He raised a hand and let it fall. 'I've been a fool.'

Fighting back her anger, she injected frost into her voice to say, 'I forgot, Mr Newman, you have the monopoly on truth around here. Honest Jake! Ha!'

'And what's that supposed to mean?' His eyes glittered with a dangerous light.

'Don't pretend you don't know! I can see through that act of yours now. I suppose I'm not surprised to have noticed the fact that you didn't bother to mention the imminent arrival of your *friend* in England. What a pity she turned up a day early. I'm sure you had some story lined up to explain her away. Or were you just going to disappear with her for a day or two?'

'Why the hell should I mention her to you? I know a lot of people you don't. You expect me to keep you informed of all their movements in and out of the country?'

'Oh, I'm sure you know a lot of people. Most of them women!'

'Some.' He was wooden-faced. 'Why the hell not? You're saying I need a licence from you?'

'Damn you, Jake Newman!' She wanted to hit him, but didn't dare. 'I'm just the girl who mucks out your horses. I don't count. I'm fair game. I hate you!'

'When I asked you to act possessive, I never counted on this. Look, Tamsin,' he ground out, 'I never made any promises.'

'That's true, at least,' she replied bitterly. 'No doubt your promises were all made in America, but you didn't have the decency to let me know!'

'If you mean Mary-Lou, you can leave her out of this. I won't have you dragging her name in the mud——'

'Loyal as well as honest!' she mocked.

'To my friends, yes, I hope I am loyal to them.'

'And what about me? What about your employees? Aren't you loyal to them?'

'Yes, I think Olley and Lin would say so. Ask them yourself.' His deliberate avoidance of the question of loyalty to herself brought a fresh tirade of abuse to her lips, astonishing even herself at this evidence of pent-up emotion. Jake listened for a moment with cold hostility before turning abruptly to the door.

'I don't have to listen to this. When you've calmed down, you can come and apologise. I shall be at the house. I trust you'll find everything you need to prepare a meal for yourself here this evening. You needn't bother to walk the dogs. Mary-Lou and I will see to them before supper. And, Tamsin,' he gave a look that shrivelled her, 'I still have the letter Emile wrote to you. And, despite all this, I'm still willing to spare you the humiliation of being turned over to the police. Your outburst just now can only be due to a sense of guilt. I would beg you to think hard about your involvement with de Monterrey and where you want to go from here.'

He was at his most English. Restrained, exact, untouchable. Her tirade had given him entirely the wrong impression. It was as if he had been turned to marble by the white heat of her outburst.

Confused by the unfamiliarity of her emotions, she could only gasp. 'Jake, please——' She stumbled forward, one hand outstretched. 'I can't bear this—I—please . . .'

He was standing upright beside the door. When she reached him, she put up her fingers to touch his lips. He didn't move. Even when she reached up on tiptoe and pressed her lips against his there was no response.

She stepped back. 'Oh, Jake . . . what's happening to us?'

'I suggest you get some rest.' With no glimmer of forgiveness in the clean-cut authority of his bearing, he swivelled to leave, and she heard the slam of the outer door as he went outside.

Later, when she picked up the phone with the wild idea of begging Emile to tell Jake he had forced her to take part in his scheming, she heard the continuous buzz telling her the phone had been re-routed to the house.

It was as sure a sign as any that his trust in her had gone for good.

CHAPTER NINE

SAYING goodbye to Lin at the top of the lane that evening, she saw Jake and Mary-Lou running alone the front of the house with the dogs.

'They're like an advert for pedigree pet food,' she observed caustically. Mary-Lou looked a million dollars in a pair of emerald cords and a casual fur-lined jacket, her blonde hair the exact shade of the labradors' glossy coats.

Alone in the flat, she changed out of her own work clothes into a fluffy jumper and a velvet skirt the colour of cognac. As she brushed out her hair and applied fresh make-up, her thoughts flew continually to Jake and Mary-Lou. Was he kissing her this very minute in the privacy of the woods? Mary-Lou didn't look the type to object.

When she heard them return, she went to the kitchen window and pretended to be rinsing something under the tap so she could look out. By contrast with Mary-Lou's gold and silver glow, Jake looked positively saturnine. As he shepherded his companion ahead of him into the house, he glanced towards the window, but Tamsin melted back out of sight.

Later, with the curtains firmly drawn and the sound of the television turned up, she made an effort to blot them both out. But one programme followed another, and for all Tamsin could tell they might have been in Chinese.

At about half-past nine she went back into the kitchen to make herself a drink, but in reality to torture herself with speculations about the goings-on across the courtyard.

Without switching on the light, she peered suspiciously between the slats of the venetian blinds. The white walls opposite glimmered in the darkness, but there were no other lights apart from a single lantern above the porch. Then she noticed that Jake's sports car had gone. It didn't make her feel any better to realise that all the time she was brooding in front of the TV they were out somewhere—together.

A wave of hopelessness engulfed her. Having made a mess of things here, maybe she should cut her losses and go back to Chantilly? Tell Emile she'd failed, and ask for her old job back? Try to pretend this horrible interlude had never taken place?

Even as the thought came into her head, she knew it was impossible. She had discovered too much about Emile by now to work for him again, and the memory of his brown fingers turning her face up to his made her shudder.

Some time after midnight, Jake's car purred up the drive. Tamsin was lying in bed and heard it even though his foot must have scarcely touched the accelerator. There was a surreptitious sound of lowered voices, the click of two carefully closed car doors, the crunch of footsteps on gravel. Burying her hot face in the pillow, she tried to make her thoughts follow a different track, but they wouldn't, and she was forced to imagine Jake's arm round Mary-Lou's waist, and the look he would give her as they entered the empty house.

Lights came on, a ground-floor light, yellowish, then the unmistakable pink glow from a bedroom. She lay in the darkness looking up at the reflection on the ceiling. Soon she would know the exact moment when Jake reached out to switch it off...

An alarm was belling through the flat like a fire warning. She lay still for a moment, then came to with a jolt. Had she slept soundly through the night, after all?

Leaping out of bed, she pulled on a towelling robe and made for the bathroom. A tantalising aroma of breakfast arose from the direction of the kitchen when she emerged, and hastily throwing on a few clothes she hurtled downstairs. The scene that met her gaze made her heart do a triple somersault.

Jake, looking as if he'd been awake for hours, was sitting in his usual chair, eating breakfast and opening his mail. He was alone.

She examined his face closely, as if searching for clues to what had gone on the night before. 'Are you working this morning?' she asked, unable to keep the note of surprise out of her voice. He was in his usual cords and jodhpur boots.

'Naturally.' He looked at her as if she were mad to think otherwise.

She eyed him warily. 'I thought——' She bit her lip. 'In the circumstances I assumed you'd be having the day off.'

'Whatever for? You haven't forgotten the show in Geneva next week, have you? I'm hardly likely to take time off at this point—for any reason.'

Unable to stop herself she blurted, 'But what about Mary-Lou?'

'I expect she's having a lie in.' His expression plainly told her it was none of her business.

Not daring to look at him, she forced herself to say, 'I suppose she'll be going with you. To Geneva, that is.' In the silence before his reply, she took a piece of toast from the rack and started to butter it without looking at him.

'She won't.' He paused. 'But you will.'

She gasped, and he added with quiet menace, 'Emile will be there, won't he? A major event like that. Later this morning you're going to ring and fix it with him.'

A confusion of emotions assailed her—relief that at least she and Jake would be together, and fear at coming face to face with Emile, with Jake and an army of Swiss police waiting to pounce.

'Are you going to make me meet him?'

His dark eyes lazed over her pale face. 'Does it bother you?'

She shook her head. Clutching at straws, she tried to feel glad—at least they would be free of Mary-Lou!

They worked the horses together all morning, but Jake was abrupt, addressing her only when necessary, just as he had before their truce. His face had that bruised, shuttered look she'd noticed before. She put it down to tiredness after the debauchery of the previous night.

'Tamsin!' A lean hand suddenly gripped her by the shoulder and she nearly fell off poor Satan.

'You're useless in this mood. Can't you concentrate for five minutes together?' His face scowled into hers. He was sitting hunched forward in the saddle watching her reaction, and, having gained her attention, sat back with both hands resting lightly on Chelsea's withers. The horses, glad of a brief rest, nuzzled each other like lovers.

Her cheeks blazed as if he had read her thoughts.

'Well?' he prompted. 'What's up?'

'It's obvious, isn't it?' she answered with a tight smile.

'You're sitting there like a sack of potatoes, that's what's obvious. And it's doing Satan no good at all. Get down and have a rest.' When she didn't react, he asked more gently, 'Am I working you too hard?' Not waiting for an answer, he went on, 'You look worn out. Go and give Lin a hand with Lord and Lady.'

'Whatever for?' she asked. 'They're not going anywhere, are they?' Lord and Lady were a couple of two-year-olds, not yet ready to join the other horses on the show-jumping circuit.

'They could be. Mary-Lou's thinking of buying them. They may as well look smart.'

She gaped at him without speaking.

'I'm worried about you,' he remarked, scrutinising her expression before riding Chelsea back on to the track. When he circled back, she was still reined in at the same spot. 'Go on, will you? I mean it. You're looking washed out.'

'Probably by contrast to Mary-Lou,' she replied tonelessly.

'Possibly,' he agreed. 'That's quite a tan she's got ... Very bad for the skin. Don't you do that to yourself.'

'Chance would be a fine thing,' she replied, confused by the inflection of concern in his voice—as if he cared what happened to her skin!

'Go on, now. Do as you're told.' He turned back towards the jumps.

'So she's thinking of buying these two, is she?' panted Tamsin a little later as she helped Lin brush the coats of the two youngsters till they shone like polished chestnut. 'I can't imagine what she thinks she's going to do with them,' she went on, stopping only to push her hair back out of her eyes.

Lin looked up. 'They've got a lot of potential,' she reproved.

'I don't mean that,' Tamsin broke in. 'I know they're good, otherwise Jake wouldn't have bothered with them in the first place. I mean—her. What on earth's she going to do with a couple of top-class show-jumpers?'

Lin looked baffled. 'Don't you know who she is?'

'Should I?'

Lin shrugged. 'Maybe not. After all, you've been off the scene for a while.'

'Don't keep me in suspense!' Tamsin exclaimed sarcastically.

Lin laughed. 'Last year she just happened to be winner of the Florida Open, that's all. And this year,' she went on while Tamsin absorbed this news with a poker face, 'she's strongly tipped to be picked for the American team in Europe.'

'Oh, no—Mary-Lou Wilmott. *That* Mary-Lou. I never guessed——' Tamsin's house of cards collapsed. 'So she and Jake have quite a lot in common,' she said at last.

'Quite a lot,' agreed Lin, unperturbed by the thought.

Tamsin hid her face behind a fall of hair and paid extra attention to Lord's coat. 'She's got just about everything anybody could want,' she said at last in a muffled voice.

'She's OK,' replied Lin generously. 'I like her.'

Suddenly Tamsin could stand it no longer. With a sudden swift kick, she slammed her booted foot hard against the side of the metal bucket at her feet. It clanged violently against the side of the stable wall, making Lady skitter just as Lin was finishing with the brush. Managing to catch hold of her head collar before she could get away, she was giving Tamsin an astonished glance when Jake came storming across the yard. His face was like a thundercloud.

'Tamsin! Are you out of your mind? I saw that! It was deliberate!'

She gave one startled glance, then, without knowing quite what possessed her, took to her heels like a frightened rabbit and began to run.

'Come back here!' he yelled. When she paid no heed, he turned to Lin, 'What the devil's going on?'

Lin's reply was lost as Tamsin ran blindly up the lane away from the stables towards the house.

Still shouting, Jake sprinted after her and caught her before she could get far. She felt his hand come down to grasp the back of her sweater, then his other hand wrapped itself tightly around her body, forcing her to halt.

'What the hell's got into you?' he demanded roughly, pinning her arms to her sides. 'You bawl me out for no reason at all, and now you're taking it out on the horses——'

'I didn't touch your stupid horses!' she shouted. 'And take your filthy hands off me.'

'No, I damn well won't until——'

'Get off me!' she snarled. 'You don't own me——'

'Not yet,' he replied cryptically.

Unable to withstand his unbearable closeness, she lashed out with a sudden kick, catching him a nasty blow on the shin. It brought a reflex of tears to his

eyes, but he started to laugh. 'You vicious little
animal,' he muttered. 'Some kitten you are!' To
her astonishment, he gathered her up in his arms
and began to run back with her as easily as if she
were a bundle of feathers towards the yard.

'Put me down!' she shrieked as soon as she got
over her surprise, but he ignored her, simply
laughing, and saying ominously,

'There's only one way to cool you down,
madam!'

Conscious of the interested faces over the tops
of the stable doors, she writhed about, in a futile
attempt to loosen his grip.

'I hate you, Jake Newman! Put me down, will
you?'

'Ask properly, like a nice little girl, if you know
what one is,' he panted.

'Not on your life!' she fumed. 'Put me down
now, you horrible man!'

'I'll put you down, all right!' His eyes shone with
what she suddenly saw as dangerous glee.

Then, out of the corner of her eye, she noticed
where he was taking her. 'No, Jake! You wouldn't!
No!'

'Yes, Tamsin, yes, I would,' he mocked.

Clawing desperately at his shoulders, she tried
now to cling on to him, and for a second, as he
changed position the better to do what he had in
mind, his warm face brushed against her own and
he was lookinmg straight into her eyes. Then, with
a lurch and a shout of triumph, he let her go.

There was a confusion of arms and legs as she
hung vainly on to his sleeve, then there was a splash
as she hit the water of the horse-trough.

It wasn't very deep, but the impact sent a cascade
of icy drops splashing up inside her T-shirt, then

she was caught in the backlash as the water surged against the sides. Stunned, she could only sit there for a moment, conscious of the hoots of laughter from everyone in the yard.

With a cry of fury she began to scrabble her way over the edge. But Jake hadn't finished yet. With a demonic grin he grasped the coiled hose from beside the stand pipe and, turning the tap, ran out a foot or two in his hands. Fascinated, Tamsin saw it wriggle to life like a long brown snake, then a jet of water shot through the air in a great silver arc. The impact stopped her breath for a minute and she stood, paralysed, one foot in the trough, the other hanging over the side, unable to believe it was really happening.

'Have you cooled down yet, or do you want more?' shouted Jake across the yard, playing the jet of water all around her as she climbed out, and making her jump from side to side in her efforts to avoid it.

Amid hoots from the stable lads, she screamed, 'Stop it! Stop it!'

But he merely played the jet on her again shouting, 'Say "Please, Mr Newman", then I might!'

Without looking down, she could feel her nipples hardening under the cold douche, and she knew they were beginning to stand out beneath the clingy fabric of her T-shirt. She saw Jake notice too, for his expression changed. 'Say please,' he challenged in a different tone. 'That's all you have to do.' He played the jet at her feet.

'I hate you, Jake Newman!' Sobbing with rage, she ducked her head and ran as fast as she could to the safety of the tack-room.

To her amazement, Lin was doubled up inside the doorway. 'Quick, Tam, in here!' She grabbed Tamsin by the arm and pulled her inside, slamming the half-door behind her. She was in hysterics.

'It's not funny!' fumed Tamsin. 'He really has it in for me!'

'Of course he hasn't! The lads are always chucking each other in there. Everybody has to go through it some time. They've had Jake himself in more times than he's had hot dinners. I'm only surprised you've got away with it for so long!'

'Well, I think it's h-horrible!' She shivered. 'I really h-hate him.' She risked another peep round the door again, to judge whether she could make a dash for the house. Jake was calmly washing down the cobblestones as if he hadn't a care in the world.

'I'm going back to the f-flat to get changed.'

She was just about to make a break for it when there was a call from the direction of the paddock gate. Leaning over the top of the door she saw Mary-Lou, immaculate in tight, white trousers and a matching top, come sauntering into the yard with a cheerful smile for everyone. Momentarily distracted, Jake turned to greet her. It was Tamsin's chance. She was nearly half-way towards the lane before Jake noticed her come out. With a yell he turned the hose after her, making her jump and dodge as she sprinted frantically out of range.

She ran between the beech hedge, great heaving sobs shaking through her. Even when she reached the flat, out of breath and shivery with cold, she was still sobbing. It was a dry, rasping convulsion she could do nothing to control. This must be the end. Clearly Jake thought nothing of her at all. Could she imagine him subjecting Mary-Lou to

such imbecile treatment? No, she couldn't, despite
the other woman's good-natured high spirits.

Rapidly peeling off her jeans and T-shirt, she
dropped them in a heap at the bottom of the stairs
while she scurried up to run a hot shower.

It was a sound in the hall that alerted her and,
regardless of the water spraying everywhere, she ran
to the door to look down. Jake was there, holding
her wet T-shirt in his hand. He saw her as soon as
she poked her head round the door. With a shout,
he began to run up the stairs two at a time.

Stifling a gasp, Tamsin shrank back, slamming
the bathroom door and grappling for the key. When
it was safely locked, she went to stand under the
shower again.

'Tamsin! Are you all right? Lin said you were in
tears.' He rattled the door.

'Go away!' Her voice came out tight with misery.

'Tamsin, open up, come on!'

'You must be joking!' A sob, the aftermath of
the earlier ones, unexpectedly shook through her.

He must have heard it, for his rattling of the door
increased. 'Are you really upset?' he demanded in
a mystified voice. 'It was only a bit of horse-play,
and you can't say you haven't been asking for it!'

'I hate you, you horrible, insensitive brute!' she
shouted above the gushing water.

'You asked for it. Kicking out like a nasty little
pony,' he informed her, with no sign of remorse.
'Creatures like you need to be taught a lesson.'

'I hate you, Jake Newman.'

'You're becoming repetitive.'

'And I never want to see you again. Humiliating
me like that! Just go away and leave me alone!'

'Fat chance!' he replied, suddenly losing
patience. 'Open this blasted door and let me have

a look at you. I can't believe a word you say. You're probably laughing your head off in there. Now come on! Open up! Do as you're told for once.'

In answer, Tamsin merely turned the shower full on. He would be able to hear it, swishing down and drumming loudly against the metal sides of the Swedish shower cubicle.

'Tamsin?' There was a warning note in his voice which she would have heeded if there hadn't been a good solid door between them. He rattled it without effect.

'Tamsin, I know you can hear me. You're not going to get away with this. It's about time somebody schooled some sense into you—you're still that hoity-toity little brat on a pony underneath your grown-up exterior.'

'Shut up, brute!' He wasn't the only one who could name-call. And, as he couldn't get at her, she could say what she liked. Her transformation when she had felt all dewy-eyed with love had been short-lived. Now she was ready to bite and scratch, if need be. Another sob shook through her.

'You *are* crying...' His voice seemed to come nearer. 'Listen, I'm going to count to three. Tamsin? Are you listening?'

'Go away!' she snarled. 'Count to a million for all I care!'

'That's your last chance! I'm coming in.'

There was a short silence in which she just had time to wonder if he had gone away, then there came a huge bang, accompanied by the sound of splintering wood. The bathroom door burst like a paper bag, and Jake, impelled by the force of his attack, hurtled into the room.

Tamsin, inside the shower cubicle, was transfixed.

He ripped the curtain aside, then faltered for a moment as her rosy nakedness was displayed to his gaze. Then he lunged forward to grasp her wrists.

Any hope of escape was out. She didn't stand a chance. But he got himself wet in the process of attempting to drag her out, and they stood blinking at each other through the water falling like rain between them. He turned her face up to his.

'You really were crying,' he observed in astonishment. For a moment he didn't seem to know what to do, but the rage that had sent him crashing through the door faded, and suddenly the wide, tanned smile took its place. 'You sweet little creature!' he exclaimed. 'All spite and snarl, but underneath as soft as a kitten!'

Then his eyes roamed helplessly over the rest of her naked form. 'Hell, Tamsin,' his voice became gruff, 'I'm sorry—but, oh hell, you look like a water nymph.' He reached out and wordlessly touched the long, wet tendrils of hair, lifting a lock between his fingers, and slowly, his eyes never leaving hers, lifted it to his lips and kissed the tip.

There was a dazed look on his face and he didn't speak.

Suddenly it seemed right that his dark, wet head should be bending over her, and then that his lips should course along her collarbone, melting into her wet, warm skin until she could feel no separation between the fingers of water pressing her limbs and the swooning touch of his male fingers probing her vertebrae with little whorls and vibrations of their own.

With a small groan deep in his throat, he leaned forward and tenderly brought her face within kissing distance. All the hard anger that had bulged his muscles gradually disappeared, leaving them heavy with another emotion, and the lines of force on his face relaxed and his body began to melt sensually against her own.

For a moment they both seemed suspended in time, like figures in a painting, then with infinite care he led her from under the falling water and pulled her down gently beside him on to the soft, deep pile of the bathroom carpet.

Tamsin gasped at the touch of his hands as they slid over her steamy skin. 'I ought to fight you,' she whispered, unable to stop herself arching against his loving touch.

'You should fight? That's rich,' he murmured, teasing a trail of kisses wonderingly over her breasts. She felt her stomach tighten in a spasm of longing as he splayed her legs and brought his weight down gently on to her. 'You've done enough fighting for one day. It's loving time now,' he went on thickly. His hands slid up to cover her breasts, making her gasp with the pleasure to come. In an instant he had transformed her into a flame fluttering beneath his touch. Her desire flared up to consume them both, and she gripped his shoulders hard as he plunged his head down to gorge himself like a starving man on a pot of sweet honey.

'I must fight you.' She shuddered, taunted by the events of the last few hours when his love seemed lost forever. But the fevered tide of longing warred against her doubts, and little by little she felt all resistance ebb. Shocked, she couldn't help but thrill to the fervour of his clear desire as he drew her down beneath him, freeing himself from the restraints of his clothes as he brought her rippling against his nakedness.

With a small, last-ditch cry of protest, she tried to wriggle free, feverish with the realisation that it

must be she who called things to a halt before they
went any further.

'Don't stop me, Tamsin,' he muttered hoarsely,
guessing what she was hoping to do. 'Come to me—
come to me...' He tried to persuade her back into
his arms till she was crushed in half surrender, his
mouth muffled in her red-gold hair as he whispered, 'Love me, Tamsin, love me——'

But memory of her previous night's anguish made
her stiffen against him. 'How can you ask that,
Jake?' She fought in his arms, scratching and
struggling, crying, 'How can you, how can you?
You want to make me love you, but you don't care
about me at all!' She tried to get away, but he held
her tight.

'What are you saying, kitten?' In thrall to her
naked beauty, he scarcely lifted his head for a reply,
but brought his lips down again and again to her
creamy skin, murmuring between kisses, 'You've
twisted me around your little finger... ever since
the day you arrived here... now start loving me for
a change... stop pretending we aren't meant for each
other...'

In a panic of fear, on the edge of losing her last
grip on sanity, Tamsin increased her efforts to get
away, knowing he could make her resistance spiral
down into nothing with one touch of his cheating
lips.

'Never! Never! Never!' Nails flashed across his
face, leaving four tracks of blood.

Stunned, he jerked open his eyes then grabbed
her fingers, crumpling them in one hand and forcing
her arm behind her back. They were both panting
now with a fever of emotion, his words rapping out
between deep plunging breaths, rasping, 'Why,
Tamsin? Why do that?'

Watching his blood bead before beginning to trickle down the unblemished hollow of his cheek, she wanted to cry out at having hurt him, but the cruelty with which he had flaunted another love in front of her hardened her heart, and she could not allow herself to give in to remorse.

'You deserve far more,' she gasped. 'How can you treat me like this? Don't my feelings count at all?'

'What? All this because you got your come-uppance at last? A drop of water? It shows you belong to Brantingham now...and to me!' Ignoring the blood trickling slowly down his chin, he held her face solemnly between his hands, gazing down at her and considering the violence she was still ready to unleash should he slacken, adding for good measure, 'I'm glad I threw you in the water— you looked magnificent...like an avenging mermaid——'

'I don't mean that,' she faltered, trying to avoid his velvety glance. 'I could have taken that as a joke any other time. But coming after last night when—when...' She closed her eyes for protection against the enervating softness of his look. 'Don't pretend you don't know what I mean, Jake. Don't pretend.'

When one movement of his would have her tipping over the edge of the abyss, she prayed she could hang on to her self-control long enough to get away. But Jake was bewildered by what she had just said, and had no intention of letting her go.

'Last night?' he queried.

'Do you think I'm blind?' she almost choked. 'I know you spent the night with her!'

His face blanched. 'With Mary-Lou?' Incredulously he gazed down at her, then his eyes began to crinkle. 'Oh, kitten, kitten, is that the explanation for today's explosion?'

She couldn't believe the evidence of her eyes. 'You're going to deny it!' Her voice was brittle with disbelief.

'You bet I am!'

Her astonished laugh was cut short when, still imprisoning her arms, he dragged her to her feet and began to push her along the corridor to his room. The door nearly flew off its hinges as he smashed it wide so she could look inside. 'Did I stage-manage this for you before I went out this morning?' he demanded.

She gaped at the unmade single bed confronting her. 'It doesn't prove anything——' she managed to stutter.

'To a nasty, suspicious mind like yours, no, it probably doesn't. If I'd realised you were the jealous type, I would have had a video camera rigged up. You could have had filmed proof of me getting my full six hours! Alone!' he added for good measure.

Despite his humorous tone, his eyes had a wary look in them, as if wondering whether she was even now going to believe him. But Tamsin was silent. She knew the room hadn't been like this yesterday evening, because she had been in here to put his clothes away after she had tidied up the sitting-room.

Wild colour flooded her cheeks. Had she misjudged him, then? She turned to speak, then hurriedly averted her glance, aware all of a sudden that both of them had discarded their clothing. Jake's desire had not slackened, and before she could back away into the safety of her own room, away from the warm, brown-eyed look he was giving her now, she felt him bring one of his hands up to smooth the tangle of damp hair from her face.

'Believe me?' he asked huskily.

'I didn't hear you come back last night,' she whispered, still unable to collect her scattered thoughts, unable, try as she might, to ignore the spinning desire his touch effected.

'You didn't hear me? Of course you didn't,' he said. 'I knew you were over-tired, so I tried not to wake you——'

'But you spent the whole evening with her——' she began.

'And you put two and two together and made nine.'

'But she's so attractive. Any man would want her...'

'She's a lovely lady and I adore her, but all that bubbly nonsense soon palls. We're simply great friends, as I told you, and we've never been anything else.'

'Oh, Jake...I hated feeling the way I did.' She spoke slowly, trying to make sense of feelings new to her. 'Is this what jealousy is? If so, it's horrible!'

'You're going to have to make a leap of faith and learn to trust me,' he told her.

'If I do,' she said slowly, a catch in her throat, 'do you think you can make the same blind leap for me, too?'

He hesitated for a moment before saying, 'Despite everything, I think a part of me always has...the question is not whether I trust you, but whether I ought to trust myself...'

Without explaining further, he began to draw her into the protection of his arms, and somehow their limbs became entwined in a way which was anything but hostile. The familiar ache in the pit of her stomach told her of her unassuaged need. He saw the instant of capitulation in her eyes, but hesitated a moment longer. 'Tamsin?' He smoothed both palms over her waist, then caressed her till she felt as smooth as melted cream. 'We ought to get dressed...'

'I know.'

He let her hang against him, supporting her with the movement of his hands, kissing her mouth, lifting his lips just a little out of range so that she rose on tiptoe to reach them, a soft sigh escaping her as he brought her close.

'It's the middle of the morning,' he went on, caressing her to an ecstasy of love. 'We have to go back...' She felt him lowering her against the billowing covers on the bed, actions countering words, intention certain. 'We have to... we must go back. Darling...?' His hot mouth sought hers and found it, and the languor of the last few moments gave way to a sudden fever of wanting.

Driven by a desperation new to her, driven to be possessed by him again, she let her body announce its desires in its own way. It meant biting and scratching him, dragging him closer still as he remained poised above her for what seemed like an eternity. His deliberate delay made her writhe and cry out for the mercy of release until he came down at last, his inexorable slowness drawing out her expectations to their limits, bringing his pulsing body at long last into her own.

This time there was no one in control as their desire met head-on in an abrupt impact that left them breathless, drenched in sweat, gasping, crying aloud, depleted with cloud-burst swiftness.

'Darling ... darling kitten. Tamsin, my love ...'
He wrapped her in his arms, rocking her to and fro
in them, cradling her.

She clung to him, her heart beating with frantic
insistence, a bubble of joyful laughter rising spon-
taneously to her lips. 'I never knew ...'

'I'm sorry, angel. It's not meant to be as quick
as that ...'

'It feels so good,' she whispered between deep
recovering gulps of air, 'so good,' she giggled, 'good
to have you squashing me like this——'

He laughed and released her from his weight, but
she pulled him back. 'Don't leave me. Stay! Squash
me forever!'

'If only we could stay ...' He smothered kisses
in her hair. 'Dare you show your face in the yard
after this?'

'Will they know?' she asked.

'They'll take one look at your face——' He kissed
her eyebrows, her temples, her chin. 'One look!'
He kissed her eyes, her flushed cheeks. 'Don't,
Tamsin, don't look at me like that!'

'I want to—I want to look at you forever.'

'You make me want to——' He broke off.

'Yes?'

'You know what, you little witch ... I want to
start all over again.' He fingered the dried blood
on his cheek. 'Apart from that, you ought to pay
for what you've done.'

'Make me pay,' she murmured throatily. 'Yes,
Jake, yes.' Then, contrite, she asked, 'Does it hurt,
poor love?' Kissing each of the four little scratches,
she said tenderly, 'Poor Jake. I've hurt you. It must
hurt.'

'Terribly.' He slid his hands down over her flat stomach, making her squirm with an upshoot of desire.

'Jake!' she breathed, head thrown back, swooning helplessly to further promise. 'Yes, Jake, please, Jake...'

He groaned and dropped his head to her breasts. 'You're wicked. You'll destroy my credibility with my staff.'

She sighed. Nothing mattered. Nothing but the magic of his touch, the enchanted spell of this wonderful love.

Eventually he lifted her in his arms and carried her back into the bathroom. 'How light you are! And you have skin like vanilla ice-cream!'

The shower was still running and he pushed her into it, joining her there and enveloping her in his arms before allowing her to swish a pine-scented gel over him.

'You're so tanned,' she remarked, slicking the foaming green liquid over his chest. 'All over, too!' Shyness seemed misplaced. She was revelling in the newness of him, of such intimacy with a man, and glorying in his golden-brown perfection. 'So strong,' she murmured, kissing the ridged muscles across his shoulders. 'So perfect!' Then she looked up mischievously. 'Am I supposed to be aloof and difficult to please? I think I'm doing everything wrong, showing you how heavenly I think you are!'

'Don't stop,' he murmured, licking the wet skin of her neck. 'It's a two-way thing. Haven't I told you I adore vanilla ice-cream?'

When they dressed and went downstairs, he pulled her back before she could go outside. Looking up, she was surprised to see a determined glitter in his eyes.

'If this doesn't seem like the right moment, I'm sorry, darling, but I told you earlier it would have to be done today.'

For a moment she was confused, then her brow cleared. 'Emile, you mean? You want me to ring him?'

He nodded. 'I want you to make an assignation with him in Geneva. Tell him I'm thinking of getting rid of Golden Boy at last, but want to give him a final chance to make good. If he fails in Geneva, I shall get rid of him then. Knowing de Monterrey, he'll imagine he's got a good chance of picking him up for a song—it should be an open invitation for him to come in and do his worst.'

Swallowing hard, she turned to the phone and began to dial Emile's number.

'Speak in English when you get through. My French isn't as good as yours.'

'It'll be one of his secretaries first,' she warned him.

His face was wooden as she obtained her connection.

'*Bonjour*, Brigitte,' she began, recognising the voice at the other end. Then she gave her own name and asked to speak to Emile, half hoping he would be out. But there was no reprieve. His voice came over almost at once.

'Tamsin, my dearest, how lovely to hear your voice so soon.'

To her own ears he spent far too much time sounding delighted. Jake's face was impassive as he listened in. Briefly she explained her call, just as Jake had instructed.

'No problem, *ma belle*. I intended to be in Geneva anyway. And this is an added incentive. At last the fish bites!'

When she replaced the receiver she leaned against Jake's solid frame, needing his warmth and reassurance.

'Not bad at the lying game, angel,' he murmured into her hair.

'I may have sounded convincing, but I felt terrible.' She looked down at her hands and saw they were shaking. Jake picked them up separately and kissed them.

'Better now?'

'Ask me when this is all over,' she told him.

She hoped she was imagining it, but Jake had a strangely withdrawn expression as they made their way back along the lane to the yard.

CHAPTER TEN

THE WEEK flew by and Mary-Lou left after another day or two, the pleased owner of Lord and Lady, and leaving a warm invitation to both Jake and Tamsin to go over and stay at her home near Louisville whenever they wanted.

Each day was spent working the horses to a peak of readiness for Geneva, and Satan had come on so well that Jake was tempted to take him over too.

'I think you should. Test him out. See how he stands up to the journey and the excitement of being at a big event,' suggested Tamsin. 'Even if you don't think he's ready on the day, at least you'll have got him used to big crowds and no harm done.'

'Yes, you're probably right,' agreed Jake. 'And if he does show form,' he gave her a glance, 'one or other of us can ride him in a novice class, can't we?' He turned his mount away and was down at the end of the outdoor paddock before she could reply.

By the time she caught up with him she was out of breath. 'Did I dream it—or did you really say what I think you said?'

He smiled briefly, a restrained element in his expression. His reply was equally guarded. 'See how it goes.' He was off again before she could say anything else.

Tamsin watched him with a puzzled frown, then pushed her disquiet to one side. What was important was that she had a whisper of a chance to ride in a big show. And wasn't that what she'd always wanted?

She longed to shout it around the stables so everybody could share her happiness, but she kept it to herself, afraid people would say it was rank favouritism, or that Jake would change his mind, or Satan hurt himself and be unfit, or that it would be jinxed in some other, as yet unimagined way and her ambitions would be dashed after all.

That evening, as they strolled wearily back to the house, Jake said he was going to turn in early, their late nights were playing havoc and he had to think of himself as being in strict training, starting now.

'I'll cook from now on too,' he told her. 'I get very finicky about what I eat before a big event.'

'I'll stroll over to Rose Mead then, and see if there's a card from Saul.'

'No——' he objected at once, breaking off and giving her an embarrassed glance.

'You mean I'm still under house arrest?' she asked, astonished. It had become a private joke between them. At night he came to her room saying, 'Just checking on the prisoner.' And she would pretend to be a captive princess and he a swashbuckling pirate king, or leader of a band of brigands. It was nonsense and they usually finished up with a pillow fight.

'I hadn't thought it was still for real!' she exclaimed. 'You said you trusted me!' Two spots of burning colour showed on her cheeks.

'I did say it was myself I was afraid to trust, if you remember,' he reminded, 'besides—I don't like you walking about the countryside by yourself after dark.'

'As well,' she added pointedly.

'All right, as well,' he agreed after a slight pause.

She stood looking up at him for a long moment without speaking. What was in her mind showed plainly in her eyes, for he flexed his shoulders obstinately before saying, 'Only I know what a fool I am for you, Tamsin. This may be nothing more than a beautiful illusion. I daren't trust my own judgement right now.'

'Fair enough.' She turned away so he wouldn't see the tears suddenly sheening her eyes. 'If you don't trust me, you don't. That's all there is to it,' she said tightly. 'I'm glad I've found out.' She glanced back at him. 'I just don't see how you can think I've been pretending all this time—at night— all those nights . . .' Her throat tightened, strangling the rest of her words.

She heard him stop beside her, then she was enveloped in his arms, his lips seeking hers and the breath crushed from her body in a powerful embrace. 'Listen to me, darling . . .' His lips were in her hair. 'It's become a case not of not trusting you, but of not trusting myself.'

He gazed down at her, intense, as serious as she had ever known him. 'There's too much at stake to risk blowing it now—Olley's brother-in-law . . . his career on the line . . . And not only him. There are others involved, too.' He paused. 'Understand, please try. I wouldn't be the first chap to throw everything away for a pretty woman——'

'I hate you sometimes!' she exploded. 'I thought we had something extraordinary. How can you compare it with anything that has ever existed before?' Weren't her own feelings returned, then? She held her breath. 'Surely you can tell I'd rather die than hurt you? I thought you felt the same way about me? You know all that stuff with Emile was a mistake. I can tell you something, Jake Newman,' she went on, 'I don't want to settle for anything less than total trust. And if I can't make you love me properly, I'd rather—I'd rather set you free to find somebody you really can love!'

She swivelled out of his arms and started to walk quickly off down the lane, too shaken to cry, too aware that it had to be all or nothing.

'Tamsin! It's not like that!' He caught her up but didn't touch her. 'It's not like that,' he repeated after a minute or two. But, by the time they reached the courtyard, he still hadn't told her what it was like.

He let them both into the flat and she walked straight past him into the hall, in frosty silence. He followed her into the sitting-room and stood looking across at her while she lit the fire, drew the curtains and turned on the television. She waited for him to say something, but after a minute or two he turned and went out without a word. She heard him start the preparations for their evening meal.

It's for him to explain if I've got it wrong, she told herself as she slumped in the wine-coloured armchair and pretended to watch the news.

The showground in Geneva was electric with enthusiastic crowds the day they arrived. Flags of all the nations fluttered like brilliant butterflies at the top of a score of tall white poles, bands played, vendors hawked their wares, and television crews broadcast their commentaries in half a dozen languages to the rest of the world. The carefully tended green of the main show ring sparkled as if each blade of grass had been individually polished. The jumps shone with fresh paint. And the horses gleamed and pranced with all the pride and dreams of their owners.

Olley and Lin, accompanied by a couple of the grooms, were driving the horse-box over the Alps with Golden Boy, Chelsea and, at the last minute, Satan, on board.

Jake and Tamsin flew out the day after they left. Jake expected Emile to be in evidence, and sure enough his name was listed among the owners, with a couple of entries in each of the main events. In the big compound where the competitors stayed, close to the vast stable complex, there was a flashy caravan with 'de Monterrey' scrolled in black on the silver coaming. The narrow blinds remained lowered, however, and it was obvious no one was in residence yet.

Tamsin was relieved to find that Jake's group of caravans was on the far side of the compound, well away from Emile's contingent.

When they arrived at the ground, going straight there from the airport with their baggage, they were conducted to the compound by one of the hostesses.

After she left, Tamsin eyed up what was to be their living quarters for the next two weeks.

'The grooms have a caravan to themselves, but they often bed down in the stables,' Jake told her when she asked about the others. 'And Olley and Lin will want a van to themselves.'

'Olley and Lin?'

'Didn't you know?' He smiled faintly. 'Why do you think they're such a good team?'

She gave him a huffy glance and looked at the remaining caravan.

''Fraid so,' he remarked, following her glance. 'It would cause too much of a scandal if we suddenly split——'

'Should *I* care?'

'You look like an angry marmalade kitten.'

'Don't be patronising.'

'Abstinence difficult to cope with?' He had been true to his word. And it wasn't just frost between them now, it was permafrost.

'Work all day, sleep all night, suits me,' she bit back. 'In fact, knowing now what you really think of me, I'm glad you haven't put temptation in my way. I would only have regretted it.'

'I'm sorry, Tamsin, I have to do it this way. I'm trying to make it easy for you.'

When he said he was sorry, he sounded as if he meant it. But it didn't alter the hard facts.

'Look, come on. I'll show you the van.' He unlocked the door and ushered her inside. She was surprised at how luxurious it was.

Fitted carpet in a shade of silky beige covered the floor and most of the walls. There was every domestic convenience possible, scaled down with precision to fit into the restricted space with no loss of efficiency. There was a cooker, fridge, deep freeze and dishwasher, even a small washing machine and drier so that the riders could keep their kit in tip-top condition. A dining-table folded away when not in use, and there was a small bar, a fold-out shower, plus, of course, a loo and small fixed washbasin in a tiny washroom.

She glanced round, puzzled for a minute, until Jake went to the front and pushed open a partition, another flick of the wrist revealing a large double bed complete with pillows, sheets and duvet.

'There's also a day bed disguised as a banquette,' he told her. 'That's if you don't fancy sleeping in the same bed as me...'

'In the same bed?' She looked at him in astonishment. 'I'm not sure what I fancy just now,' she told him candidly, striving to keep her voice calm, 'but I thought you had to be single-minded about your training, so you've been telling me.'

'Training's over. This is the real thing,' he said huskily.

She stepped back, bumping against a corner of the bed. 'The real thing?'

His eyes were velvety, but she turned her head. 'It's easy enough for you to switch on and switch off when the mood takes you,' she bit out, with all the accumulated hurt of the last few days bursting to come out, 'but what do you think I am? Some sort of automatic lover you can pick up or put down at a whim? I'm a living, breathing human being, Jake. What do you think I've been feeling all this time, knowing your door was shut against me?' She began to cry, silently, hopelessly. It was as if he were taunting her with the brief tour round the little place that was to be their home for the next week. It was a perfect little love-nest. For the right couple.

He met her outburst without a word, as if, indeed, the door that was closed against her was the one that gave access to his heart.

It whipped up her feelings as nothing else could, and she gave him a look of unfeigned bitterness.

'This could be paradise,' she told him, trying to dash away the scalding tears as if they were somebody else's. 'But instead it's a mockery of the closeness I thought we had. You just don't care a damn about me. You think only about yourself. When it suited you to have a lover in your bed, you talked me into believing you really wanted me. But when it didn't suit you, you gave me this story of training. Now you feel like having me back for a day or two, so suddenly training's over!'

Jake's face had taken on a wooden look and she had no idea what he was thinking. The self-discipline he imposed on himself seemed to extend to his emotions, too. They were as well-schooled as the horses he rode.

'Let's not pursue the matter now,' he replied, turning away and shrugging on a casual jacket. 'We've both had a long day and it's time to eat.'

It was evening by the time they returned, having rounded off a meal at a waterside restaurant with a stroll by the lake. They stood in silence watching the bright lights of the ferries and the happy groups of people coming and going. Lovers wrapped in each other's arms brought home to Tamsin as nothing else could just what it was she was missing. She longed to respond to Jake's velvet glances, longed to be in his arms once more. But pride kept her aloof. She could not give in.

Floodlights were shining brilliantly over the showground from stanchions along the high, white fencing around the perimeter as they came back. They shed a metallic glare over everything, making it as bright as day but not as natural. Jake, despite her persistent rebuffs throughout the evening, was as gently attentive as before.

Security was tight, and after showing his pass he deliberately linked his arm round her waist as they sauntered back past the different foreign sections towards their own caravan. Despite his attempts to thaw the ice between them, Tamsin felt too hurt and angry to adopt a forgiving mood. Sounds of good-natured laughter and music mingled in the air, emphasising, in her mind, their own lack of accord.

As they drew level with Emile's caravan she noticed slits of light between the black and silver blinds, and she was just about to mention this to Jake when the door opened and light glared out over the path. There was an impression of black and silver and sharp-angled mirrors as they passed the door, then a voice came from a figure at the top of the steps.

'*Bonsoir et bonne chance,* Roger.' The voice was unmistakable.

Tamsin would have shrunk back into the shadows, but the lights high above illuminated the whole scene with pinpoint clarity. Emile turned and didn't even falter. He came straight down the steps in a cloud of cigarette smoke and walked straight up to Tamsin as if she had been waiting for him.

'*Ma belle!*' Before she could back away, he pulled her into his arms as though he had been longing for just this moment and started to talk rapidly in French, giving not even a cursory glance in Jake's direction.

'Emile! Emile?' She tried to move away. 'I'm with someone...'

Only then did he glance across at Jake.

'This is—this is Jake Newman,' she announced as casually as she could, at the same time wishing the ground would swallow her up, frightened that Emile would guess instantly how things stood between herself and Jake, and worried about the havoc he could wreak with one malicious remark on their already precarious relationship.

But Jake was smoothly nodding a greeting and Emile was saying, 'Emile de Monterrey,' and giving a half-bow. And the ground didn't open up, nor the thunderbolts strike. All that happened was that Jake and Emile, for all their suave smiles, failed to shake hands, and Emile said in English, 'I'm just on my way back to my hotel. We must have lunch soon, we three. Fix it with my secretary, *ma belle.* Tell me all your news then.'

And with a final flick of a smile to include Jake as well as Tamsin, he lifted a hand with a soft, *'Ciao!'* and was swallowed by the night.

'You're a cool devil,' she said, as soon as Emile had gone.

'I have to be. It goes with the job.' He was blank-faced.

'What thoughts are going through your head, I wonder?' She feared they boded no good for herself.

'That's a Pandora's box of a question, best avoided,' came the infuriating reply, as if to confirm her fears.

The memory of Emile's lips on her cheek made her bring up her knuckles and rub it to get it clean. If Jake noticed the gesture, he said nothing.

'Did we decide on the day bed and the double bed. Or just the double bed?' he asked, breaking the silence that had trailed them all the way to the caravan.

'I couldn't sleep with you tonight, Jake.'

'So it's still gnawing at you, what I said the other day?'

'What do you expect?'

He gave her a bleak glance, swiftly concealed, that would have wrung her heart if she hadn't felt so wronged.

He was already pulling at the duvet for the banquette before she could bring herself to say, 'I'd keep you awake. I'm really on edge.'

'I need as much sleep as I can get.' He gave her a brief smile. 'It's going to be a tough contest tomorrow. I'll hit the sack straight away.'

Despite his words, she could hear him tossing and turning for a long time after his hand came out to switch off the light.

From the solitary luxury of the double bed, she too lay looking up sleeplessly into the dark. Was it clutching at straws to hope he had used the ploy of abstinence in order to make things easier for her? After all, he knew how she felt about his lingering doubts.

She prayed that it was so, for her heart was slowly bleeding. She had longed to spend her days and nights with him but, now they were doing just that, they seemed further apart than ever. Everything that happened became another wedge between them.

The following day was hectic with activity. Olley and the gang arrived from England, and the condition of the horses took precedence over everything else. Tamsin was curtly told to keep out of the way, though she ignored this order to some extent, riding Satan round and round the practice ring whenever it was empty. Lin was cheery and methodical, checking and double-checking everybody's routine, clucking over Olley, whom she packed off to bed as soon as they arrived.

'The fool insisted on driving the whole way by himself,' she told Tamsin proudly, despite her words. 'He knows quite well I can handle the horse-box myself. Men, honestly!' She seemed to assume that things were back to rights between Jake and herself.

'One thing I'd like to know,' said Tamsin, 'is why everybody but me has a pass to the compound.' While Jake had accompanied her in and out of the wire-mesh gates the previous day, it hadn't occurred to her that she would be trapped, a virtual prisoner within, now that he was too busy to escort her. None of the others apparently had the power to sign her in and out.

'What does Jake say?' asked Lin.

'He hedges.'

'There's never any chance of getting sense out of him when his mind's on winning. Perhaps he's just being over-protective. Where do you want to go? Round the shops?'

Tamsin shrugged. 'Nowhere in particular. It's just the principle of the thing.' She wondered if Jake had counted on the fact that she couldn't get away. To Emile's hotel, for example.

She spent the time idling round the compound, or watching TV in the caravan. Once or twice she joined a group from some of the other caravans, and they sat in the sun on the terrace below the competitors' viewing stand, good-naturedly assessing the field.

'Newman's where I put my money,' finished up a stocky chap in a flat cap. When he went off in the direction of the bar, Tamsin asked who he was. 'I'm sure I've seen him somewhere before.'

'He's a sports writer now. But he used to ride before he had a nasty fall.' Tamsin had noticed the limp. This was one more dread to add to the other one—the show-down that was getting nearer every hour.

Lin was just debating whether to come in to have a cup of coffee with Tamsin when one of the messengers appeared, bearing an elaborate bunch of hot-house flowers done up in cellophane like a glass coffin.

'*Mademoiselle 'arland?*' he queried, looking from one to the other and finally settling accurately on the legitimate recipient of the gift he bore.

Tamsin took hold of the bouquet and looked for a card.

'There, that proves he's still thinking of you,' joked Lin. Tamsin unfolded the stiff white card, read it, then refolded it. She didn't say anything. All the time she was making coffee and later when they were sitting drinking it, the bouquet glared gaudily from the shelf where she had dropped it.

'You ought to put them in water,' Lin remarked.

'I will do later. They last for ages, these florists' specials.'

If Lin was surprised at the note of ingratitude in Tamsin's voice, she didn't comment.

Later, when she had gone and Jake had returned, looking hot and tired, she pointed to the bouquet and said, 'Now we know where he's staying.'

Jake gave it a cursory glance. 'He hasn't lost the old touch then?' He picked up the card and read it. 'Hotel Excelsior.'

He towered over her in the small saloon and, reaching down, stroked the top of her head a couple of times. 'I wonder if it'll do the trick again,' he murmured half to himself.

She flinched back, knocking his hand to one side. 'How *can* you?' She turned her head, furious with him and with her own reaction. He leaned down and gripped her by both shoulders. She could feel the heat from his hands through the thin cotton of her blouse. His face hovered just above her own. Even though he didn't say as much in words, she knew instantly what was going through his mind. But his first round in the Open was tomorrow morning. The excitement, the will to win, had been palpable for days.

'Does it always get you like this?' she asked with a bitter glance before trying to shrug off his hands.

'It?'

'Excitement at the thought of winning.'

'At the thought of you, you mean.' He was almost vibrating with energy. She could feel it sweeping over her like an electric current. If she had only been sure it was desire it would have sent her defences flying in seconds, but she clung on to the idea that it was simply the burn before the challenge. Nothing to do with her at all. She began to struggle as if he held her in a physical embrace. His hands slid loosely away from her shoulders, but it was as if he still held her by an invisible and unbreakable cord.

'Stop it, Jake. Let me go!'

'I'm not stopping you.' His voice was husky. He knew as well as she did what was happening. 'It's been so long. So unbearably long. Was it a mistake, kitten?'

'You'll find out tomorrow when you win or lose. If you win, you'll no doubt imagine it's all been a raging success. Just don't expect me to fall into your arms the minute you step down from the winner's rostrum, because I shan't. Nor shall I when you have Emile carted away by the *gendarmes*.' With an effort, she struggled to her feet and, flinching back from any further contact, stumbled outside.

With her hand on the latch, she stood in the clean, fresh Swiss air for a moment, trapped, needing to get away, and, not quite knowing where she was going, she started to trail round the compound again. When she got back later, the caravan was in darkness and a silent mound in the day bed told her that Jake was already asleep.

*   *   *

The Newman contingent were over the moon next day when Jake won the challenge trophy on Chelsea and got through to the second round in the Grand Prix on Golden Boy. Satan had stood up to the journey so well that he decided to ride him in one of the novice classes to give him his first taste of top competition. Tamsin was disappointed to find she wasn't asked, but saw the sense of Jake riding him when he was on such good form.

There were two days to go to the final.

'Two days,' remarked Jake, 'when de Monterrey will have to make a move if he still has his sights on Boy.'

Olley and the rest of them took it in turns to keep a guard on the horse at all times. Tamsin knew they thought it unsupportive of her not to take her turn too, but she left it to Jake to talk that problem away should he feel the inclination.

Satan's début was scheduled at three o'clock the next day. Tamsin hadn't seen Jake since mid-morning when she stood by herself at the rail and watched longingly as he took the great black horse over the practice fences. She went to have a drink about half-past eleven, surprised to find no familiar faces around, and when she came back Olley was rubbing Satan down in the yard outside the loose-box by himself.

'Jake was looking for you just now. He's gone into town,' he told her. 'That snake sent a message in to him, saying he wanted a word. And we all know what that's about, don't we?' Having told her that, he led Satan inside, and Tamsin wandered over to the caravan, noting that the blinds were down in the one next door, suggesting that Lin was catching up on her sleep after the previous night.

When Jake didn't appear at lunchtime, she ate a solitary meal by herself, wondering if he was still arguing it out with Emile. She didn't know what his exact plans had been, and couldn't imagine what they could be saying to each other. Maybe Emile had decided to ask Jake straight to his face if he would sell. But, after all the scheming that had gone on, that didn't seem likely.

After clearing away, she made her way back to the stables. Olley was getting Satan ready. He was perfectly turned out, with his coarse black mane done up in a row of little plaits tied with scarlet ribbons. Tamsin commented on how proud he seemed of his appearance.

'Jake's going to have to step on it. He's got to get changed yet.' Olley looked worried.

'I know. I'll go and get his things ready, shall I?' Pleased at having found some way to make herself useful, she went back to the van. To be honest, she had hoped Jake might have come back in the twenty minutes she had been away, but there was still no sign of him.

Methodically laying out his white shirt, stock and jacket on the banquette, she fetched his cap and brushed imaginary specks off it, checked his boots and put out a pair of clean socks. There seemed nothing else to do, so she went back to the stables.

'Still no sign?' Olley looked worried. 'It's not like him to leave it last minute like this.' He looked again at his watch as if he might have misread the time, then shook his head. 'Satan's raring to go. He knows something's in the air.'

Considering, he eyed the horse, then eyed Tamsin. 'I don't like it,' he said again.

Tamsin sat on a bench and waited. Her nerves were unravelling like the raw edge on a piece of silk. What if something had happened to him? What if he needed help? How ruthless was Emile? She was brought out of her reverie by Olley.

'Tamsin, here a minute.'

She went over to him, patting Satan absent-mindedly as he pranced and pulled at his head-collar.

'It doesn't look as if Jake's going to show up in time. He has to report to the check-in within five minutes, otherwise he'll lose the chance to enter Satan at all. It'd be a shame to scratch him when he's in such good shape.' He paused and gave her a level glance. 'What about it? Fancy a spin round the course yourself?'

'Me?' She was too astonished to speak, and gaped at Olley as if he had two heads.

'You'll have to make up your mind sharpish so we can get your name in as substitute rider.'

'But I can't—I mean——'

'Yes, you can. I reckon you won't show yourself up. I wouldn't suggest it if I thought you'd make us a laughing-stock.'

'Oh, Olley! It's what I've always wanted. It's what I've dreamed and prayed for...'

'Right, then. You stay with Satan. I'll get along to the desk and have you booked in. Lin'll be here in a minute, then you can go and get changed.'

Before she could object, he had started off down the long alley in the direction of the check-in.

A few minutes later she heard the announcement over the loudspeaker. It was something she had longed to hear, her own name among those of the other competitors. A buzz of interest from the crowd came clearly over the stable roof. It set her pulses racing, followed swiftly by a sick feeling in the pit of her stomach—doubts, fears, sheer nerves—then suddenly it cleared, making way for pure elation. She was going to do it! She was going to ride out, focus of a million eyes, TV cameras following her round one of the most challenging courses in Europe!

Satan had pricked up his ears now as if he knew. He was a winner of a horse. If he was going to be ready, today was the day. If he didn't freak at the sight of the vast crowd, then nothing would stop him!

Then she caught her breath. In all this, she had forgotten one thing. Jake. Her flight of fancy ground to a halt.

What if something terrible had happened to him? Nightmarish thoughts began to crowd her mind. With a shudder she knew what she had to do.

As soon as Lin came rushing up, she thrust the reins into her hands, saying, 'Listen, Lin, I've got to go——'

'No hurry,' Lin smiled. 'They haven't drawn the jumping order yet——'

'I mean, I've got to go and find Jake.' She paused and tried to gather her thoughts. 'Olley mentioned something about him having gone to meet Emile. And he's not back yet. I'm worried. *Anything* could have happened.'

'But——'

'I *must*, Lin! There's no choice.' Without bothering to explain further, she hurried off down the yard to the van. Grabbing a jacket and some loose change, she fled towards the exit. There was no end of places where they might have decided to meet, but the obvious one was the Hotel Excelsior. Knowing she was throwing aside a chance in a million, she went through the security gate. There would be problems getting back in without a pass if Jake wasn't found. But he must be. He had to be.

A tram stop was situated a few yards down the road and, boarding one with 'Stadt' emblazoned on the front, she was soon being borne towards the city.

CHAPTER ELEVEN

THE HOTEL EXCELSIOR was as grand as its name. Tamsin swept inside, undaunted by the immediate signs of ancient wealth, despite her casual denims. It was home ground of a sort, and she stood looking round for a moment with the air of one who belongs.

There was a mile of ruby-coloured carpet between the entrance and the flower-banked reception desk, and a bar lay to her left, a further bar, restaurant and coffee-shop to her right. Ahead were a series of glass doors, some of which stood open giving a view of a pearl and gold ballroom beneath a glass dome, and more banks of flowers set between clusters of white and gold tables ringing the floor. A pianist at a white grand piano was picking out a romantic melody as Tamsin stepped forward to scan the faces of the tea dancers circling the piano on its own flowery island. A lustre of silver and gold hovered in the air. But of Jake there was no sign.

Hurrying towards the bar on her left, she made another quick examination of the faces that turned towards hers, and again the same thing in the coffee-shop and restaurant without any luck.

With a feeling of disappointment she turned away and headed towards reception. If she could find out the number of Emile's suite, she would ask reception to call him up.

Tamsin listened in as the girl keyed the number and a man's voice answered at the other end.

She turned to Tamsin. 'Name?'

'Just a—a friend,' she blurted, suddenly frightened that Emile would refuse to see her. The receptionist's expression betrayed no opinion as she relayed this to Emile.

'Please go up. Suite one-zero-two.'

As she walked through reception to the lift, she noticed the TV consoles dotted around, all of them tuned to a shot of the showground, with the day's results displayed on a board in the background. It was eerie to see Jake's name. It made her feel cold, wondering what had happened to him.

She entered the lift, nerves whipped up, rather than soothed by the soporific music being piped in, with fears about what would be lying in wait for her when she got out. Then at last the lift stopped, the doors opened and she was hurrying along the thickly carpeted corridor, finding the dark mahogany door with its polished brass number plate, rapping on it with her knuckles and then giving a gasp as Emile's whiplash figure appeared instantly in the doorway.

'You!' he snarled when he saw her.

'Where's Jake?' she demanded without preliminaries, surprised to find her voice sounding so firm.

'What are you talking about? How should I know?' he hedged.

'You asked him to meet you this morning. Where is he, Emile?'

'You told him everything, you silly fool! What was the point of that?' He reached out and grasped her by the collar of her shirt, as if he'd like to strangle her.

'I have to know where he is!' she panted rapidly, clawing at his hands. His rage alarmed her, and she wondered fleetingly if a gun-shot would be audible in such a place.

'Worried that he's playing fast and loose with you already, you poor little fool?' His lip curled. 'I should have known you'd lose your head over him, but somehow I credited you with more common sense.'

'Don't be stupid, you loathsome man! What have you done to him? Where is he? Tell me, or I'll—I'll—I'll kill you, Emile! I will! Just tell me——'

'I don't think you need go quite as far as that, kitten,' drawled a voice from inside the room, and then to Tamsin's enormous relief Jake himself came strolling towards the door. Emile spun round as if expecting a knife in the back, but Jake merely put his hands in his pockets like a man with all the time in the world, and gave him a slow, judging look that contained such a threat of latent danger in it that Emile actually backed away into the corridor until Jake reached out and pulled him roughly back into the suite. Nodding to Tamsin to come inside, too, he very firmly shut the door, dropping the latch as if he expected Emile to try to make another dash for it.

The three of them stood facing each other in the narrow hall, the air crackling unbearably with the stark animosity of both men, until Jake, without saying much, somehow made them all follow him back into the spacious drawing-room across the hall.

There was someone there already. It was a woman, strikingly attractive in black and white, standing by the french windows, and she lifted her head with a little jerk of surprise when Tamsin came in.

Emile had quickly regained his composure, and now he sauntered over to a chair and sat elegantly on the arm of it, a narrow smile playing round his lips as he gazed back at Tamsin who was still standing in the doorway.

'If you had stayed with me, *ma belle*, none of this unpleasantness would have happened. I can be generous to those I can trust.'

'Stay with you—and be kept?' she couldn't stop herself from exclaiming in disgust.

Emile understood at once. 'What more can you hope for from him?' He indicated Jake, who by now was standing next to the woman near the window. 'You're surely not crazy enough to be holding out for marriage?' He gave a derisive laugh. 'He'll marry money. Not you, my poor, penniless little Miss Nobody. Don't you understand that yet?'

His words hurt. For all Tamsin knew, they were true too. But it didn't matter. Jake was safe. She felt weak all of a sudden, seeing him like this, not knowing what was going on, with wave after wave of relief overwhelming her now she knew he was here and not lying with a bullet in his head at the bottom of some hotel lift shaft. She wouldn't have put anything past Emile. Now all she could do was just stand and gaze and gaze at Jake, her heart in her mouth at what would happen next.

'Tamsin, my sweet,' Emile continued in insinuating tones, 'I can't bear to think of you being made unhappy. Remember how things were in Chantilly between us?' He gave Jake a smooth look before turning triumphantly to observe Tamsin's frozen expression. 'You wouldn't want to say goodbye to all that, would you, darling?'

'But——' she protested.

'You can see by now that nothing is forever,' he went on. 'Not even this silly misunderstanding between us.' He got up and came across the room to take hold of her hand, gripping it firmly in his before she could pull away. 'You know I will welcome you back to Chantilly, despite your little lapse with Newman. Well?' He moved closer. 'What do you say?'

He gave a smile that brought fingers of ice rippling up her spine as he half turned to indicate Jake and the mystery woman. 'As you can see, your friend Newman is in the best of spirits and never short of a beautiful companion or two.'

Actually, when Tamsin looked across at Jake and her gaze met his, he looked anything but in the best of spirits. His face was like a thundercloud. She watched his glance drop to her hand still clasped in Emile's. Then, before she could move, he turned to his companion. 'I think we can go down now. I've said all I want to say to this fellow.'

As he walked past Emile, he said casually, 'Pity those letters were such obvious forgeries. Tamsin suspected as much all along.'

Relief thudded through her, though of course she had known it had only been Emile's self-confident air that had made her doubt. Now, as she watched, Jake ushered the woman towards the door and they went out into the corridor.

'Jake!' she called, suddenly coming to life and pitching herself after him. The woman was already at the lift and the doors were opening when Jake turned to look back. The woman slipped inside and Jake, with a strange look on his face, followed. The doors closed on them both, and Tamsin was acutely conscious of Emile's soft laughter behind her.

'Ravishing, isn't she?' He was still by her side. 'She is one of the great race-horse owners of France, of course. You must have seen her at Chantilly, and in the social pages of all the top magazines. Who can blame him for falling for her?'

'Go away!' Tamsin felt like pushing Emile right through the wall and, as if guessing her feelings, he stepped hurriedly to one side. Without giving him another glance, she ran across to the stairs and began to hurry down them as fast as she could. She reached the bottom just as Jake and his companion stepped out of the lift. She saw them cross to the silver and gold ballroom, then begin to weave their way over the floor beneath the glass dome. Jake had his hand beneath the woman's elbow, and just then the pianist started to play a bittersweet melody that brought tears to Tamsin's eyes.

She hesitated on the edge of the marble ocean that divided her from the man she loved, afraid to take the plunge for the heartbreak it might bring, yet unable to live through another minute without confronting him once and for all with the truth. She was in an agony to tell him that everything Emile had implied was nothing but a malicious pack of lies.

Crying out to him in her heart, she watched as he ushered his companion through the glass doors on the far side of the room. The two dark heads and the woman's striking black and white outfit were clearly visible as they skirted the wall of french windows on the far side.

Someone tried to push past Tamsin and she stepped aside. When she looked back, she saw Jake returning. This time he was alone.

Helpless to make a move, she watched as he appeared and disappeared behind the glass panels,

then she moved forward and had just started down
the steps to the edge of the dance-floor when he
came into view at the door directly opposite. She
saw him put up his hand to push it open.

He caught sight of her then through one of the
panels. She saw him hesitate. Then the door was
opening. He was coming through it. His dark figure
was striding on to the pearly marble floor. Then
she saw his arms open. She too was moving
forward. Somehow or other they met in the middle
of the floor, and she felt his arms come round her,
gripping her tight. They rocked together. She saw
her tears cascade in little drops all over his shirt
front.

'I thought he'd killed you. Olley made me enter
Satan. Oh, Jake, I was so frightened for you!'

He looked down at her. 'Did you win?'

'Win?' She stared back. Then she gave a rueful
smile. 'I'm sorry. I came here instead.'

'Instead?' He looked astonished.

'I was so worried,' she tried to explain. Then,
oblivious to their audience, she kissed his cheek,
burying her face in his shoulder. 'Satan will have
been disqualified by now. I'm so sorry. I've let you
all down. But you're safe and that's all that
matters.' She lifted her head and couldn't help her
eyes darting to the door through which Jake had
ushered his companion a moment before. Time for
explanations later. It was enough to be here in his
arms and to be able to hold him close.

Jake himself suddenly lost the air of doubt he
had worn for so long. 'Let me get this straight,' he
said slowly. 'You had the chance to ride Satan—
but you refused...' he looked incredulous '...and
came chasing out here instead?'

'Are you angry?' For a moment she thought of all the preparations that had gone into getting Satan up to form, not to mention the expense of bringing him out to Switzerland in the first place.

'Darling kitten, angry? I think you're crazy! I thought you'd give your right arm to ride a winner?'

He held her hard against him, equally oblivious to the stares of everyone around them, stroking her hair as if she really were a kitten. 'Did Olley tell you what happened last night?'

She shook her head.

'Oh, Tamsin, I want to hold you in my arms forever. I want to tell you how much I love you. And I want you to tell me again that you turned down a chance to ride Satan and came looking for me instead. Is that what you really said?'

'Yes, Jake darling.' She smiled, happiness beginning to bubble through her like a hot spring at the sight of his dear face so close to hers. 'What did you honestly expect me to do? I thought I told you I wanted you more than anything else?'

'More than being a grown-up poppet of the Royal Enclosure?'

'More than anything in the whole, wide, wonderful world.'

He led her to a table made private by banks of orchids and palms.

'That's all I've wanted to hear ever since you started using your wiles on me, trying to win me over, flaunting your beautiful body at every turn. I felt so used, Tamsin. It was as if I only existed as a ticket to fame and fortune. I couldn't convince myself that you weren't out to get what you could out of me like so many others. And then I started to think, well, if those are her terms, I accept.

Rather that than lose you altogether. But now you've proved me wrong!'

He gripped her tightly by the hand across the table. 'Forgive me, kitten. I've wronged you. Forgive me.'

'Jake, I can understand how you felt. But,' she looked serious, 'there is something I'd quite like to ask you...'

'Anything. Ask on.'

'Well, three things,' she began. 'One, is it true the letters Emile had were forgeries?' He nodded. 'I knew it!' she exclaimed with satisfaction. 'If only I'd had the common sense to call his bluff!'

'Then we wouldn't have met,' he pointed out. 'Two?'

'Two,' she went on, wiping the sudden horror-stricken expression off her face. 'Why have you been here all day missing your class? And three——' she went on, before he could interrupt, and she blushed as she spoke, 'at the risk of sounding as jealous as I feel, who was that lady I saw you with just now?'

'Two,' he began, 'last night one of Emile's stable-lads was caught red-handed, breaking into Boy's stall. When searched, the police found him in possession of a nasty substance which, I'm told, is not only illegal, but harmful to horses as well. Not unnaturally, your friend de Monterrey——'

'My friend?'

Jake smiled. 'Your ex-employer—was worried by this, especially as the lad blurted out everything he knew. De Monterrey hoped he'd be able to talk me into not pressing charges. Hence his note this morning.'

'And did he?'

'I'm afraid it was all rather taken out of my hands. The show committee are bringing charges. It's going to be the end of de Monterrey for a while.' He gave her a wide dazzle of a smile. 'If you were thinking of taking up his offer to resume things in Chantilly, I'm afraid you're in for a disappointment.'

'Jake Newman, if you ever say anything like that to me again I'll——'

'Kiss me?' He held her hand across the table, even when the waiter brought a pot of coffee. He handed a note to Jake at the same time as he set the tray down.

'Three,' he resumed, glancing at the note and continuing, 'my companion just now was the owner of the horse Olley's brother-in-law rode at Newmarket last year. The one that was doped, remember? We got together on this, and now it's up to her and the jockey club as to what happens to him after the Swiss authorities have finished with him. And four——'

'I didn't ask four.'

'Four. I love you, darling kitten, even if you are a gullible little fool and require a firm hand, and what's more, I'm willing to risk being scratched to bits if you'll put me out of my misery and marry me.'

'Jake, do you think I'll say no?'

'It is possible.'

'And Satan might sprout wings and fly. Of course I'll marry you. But I haven't got a fortune. And Emile says that's what you want?'

'I've got enough to keep the pair of us, plus a couple of thoroughbreds, and two or three children's ponies should the need arise. And it won't matter if I'm a pauper anyway, because I'm going to set you to work for me. You're going to ride my horses and make a fortune.'

'Oh, Jake...'

'Oh, Tamsin...' He flicked a look at his watch and half rose. 'Look here, if we don't get a move on you'll miss your class.'

'My class?'

'If you had a choice, which would you prefer, tea and cream buns here, or a crack at the cup on Satan?'

'If I had a choice, I guess I could live without the cream buns. Anything, just so long as I don't have to live without you.' She smiled trustingly up at him.

'Come on, then!' Grasping her by the arm, he began to hurry her through the dancers towards the doors.

'What? Wait—I——'

'Don't argue. A message has just come through. The novice event has been delayed due to some bureaucratic bungle. You still have time to get out there and show us what you can do!'

Tamsin didn't argue. Tea forgotten, they drove straight back to the showground. Satan, despite his name, behaved like an angel—and, exactly as everyone had predicted, he and Tamsin rode in a triumphant first.

Later, at the celebrations that night, Jake stood up to announce their engagement.

'Not before time,' Olley was heard to mutter as glasses clinked and congratulations rang out.

'The same might be said of you, my friend,' smiled Jake, placing a hand on his shoulder.

Olley grinned sheepishly at Lin. 'Well, what about it, old girl? Boss's orders.' Jake made him propose properly and more champagne was called for, a band struck up and people started to dance.

At a respectably early hour Jake turned to Tamsin with a rueful smile and told her they would have to leave. 'Big event tomorrow. Need my sleep.'

'I'm feeling sleepy, too,' agreed Tamsin readily.

'You'll feel even sleepier after tonight if you run true to form,' he murmured, nibbling her earlobe as he unlocked the door of the caravan.

'But what about your class tomorrow?' she murmured in mock surprise as she sank into his arms and he started to undress her. 'Aren't you still in training, Mr Newman?'

'I only said that to make it easier for you, you know,' he told her, serious for a moment. 'I knew how much you hated not being trusted, but I couldn't risk trusting you completely, there were too many people depending on me. And I couldn't tell you everything in case you accidentally gave the game away when Emile started questioning you. And anyway,' his tone changed, 'what do you mean, tomorrow? You must mean the day after. Tomorrow's my day off!'

He pulled her down on to the double bed beside him. 'Now, marmalade, where were we?'

'Big event?' she queried, slithering up against him and pulling at his buttons.

'Tomorrow,' he told her, 'we're going to do some shopping. I nearly punched Emile when I saw him pawing you this afternoon. And just so it doesn't happen again, with anyone, we'll let diamonds do the trick. What do you think?'

'A bridle ring would do if it came from you,' she murmured, smothering his reply as she pulled his head down to hers and their lips met. Safe in his arms at last, she knew love like theirs needed no other bond to make it last forever.

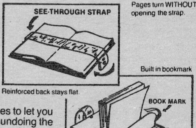

PASSPORT TO ROMANCE VACATION SWEEPSTAKES

OFFICIAL RULES

SWEEPSTAKES RULES AND REGULATIONS. NO PURCHASE NECESSARY.
HOW TO ENTER:

1. To enter, complete this official entry form and return with your invoice in the envelope provided, or print your name, address, telephone number and age on a plain piece of paper and mail to: Passport to Romance, P.O. Box #1397, Buffalo, N.Y. 14269-1397. No mechanically reproduced entries accepted.

2. All entries must be received by the Contest Closing Date, midnight, December 31, 1990 to be eligible.

3. Prizes: There will be ten (10) Grand Prizes awarded, each consisting of a choice of a trip for two people to: i) London, England (approximate retail value $5,050 U.S.); ii) England, Wales and Scotland (approximate retail value $6,400 U.S.); iii) Caribbean Cruise (approximate retail value $7,300 U.S.); iv) Hawaii (approximate retail value $ 9,550 U.S.); v) Greek Island Cruise in the Mediterranean (approximate retail value $12,250 U.S.); vi) France (approximate retail value $7,300 U.S.).

4. Any winner may choose to receive any trip or a cash alternative prize of $5,000.00 U.S. in lieu of the trip.

5. Odds of winning depend on number of entries received.

6. A random draw will be made by Nielsen Promotion Services, an independent judging organization on January 29, 1991, in Buffalo, N.Y., at 11:30 a.m. from all eligible entries received on or before the Contest Closing Date. Any Canadian entrants who are selected must correctly answer a time-limited, mathematical skill-testing question in order to win. Quebec residents may submit any litigation respecting the conduct and awarding of a prize in this contest to the Régie des loteries et courses du Quebec.

7. Full contest rules may be obtained by sending a stamped, self-addressed envelope to: "Passport to Romance Rules Request", P.O. Box 9998, Saint John, New Brunswick, E2L 4N4.

8. Payment of taxes other than air and hotel taxes is the sole responsibility of the winner.

9. Void where prohibited by law.

PASSPORT TO ROMANCE VACATION SWEEPSTAKES

OFFICIAL RULES

SWEEPSTAKES RULES AND REGULATIONS. NO PURCHASE NECESSARY.
HOW TO ENTER:

1. To enter, complete this official entry form and return with your invoice in the envelope provided, or print your name, address, telephone number and age on a plain piece of paper and mail to: Passport to Romance, P.O. Box #1397, Buffalo, N.Y. 14269-1397. No mechanically reproduced entries accepted.

2. All entries must be received by the Contest Closing Date, midnight, December 31, 1990 to be eligible.

3. Prizes: There will be ten (10) Grand Prizes awarded, each consisting of a choice of a trip for two people to: i) London, England (approximate retail value $5,050 U.S.); ii) England, Wales and Scotland (approximate retail value $6,400 U.S.); iii) Caribbean Cruise (approximate retail value $7,300 U.S.); iv) Hawaii (approximate retail value $ 9,550 U.S.); v) Greek Island Cruise in the Mediterranean (approximate retail value $12,250 U.S.); vi) France (approximate retail value $7,300 U.S.).

4. Any winner may choose to receive any trip or a cash alternative prize of $5,000.00 U.S. in lieu of the trip.

5. Odds of winning depend on number of entries received.

6. A random draw will be made by Nielsen Promotion Services, an independent judging organization on January 29, 1991, in Buffalo, N.Y., at 11:30 a.m. from all eligible entries received on or before the Contest Closing Date. Any Canadian entrants who are selected must correctly answer a time-limited, mathematical skill-testing question in order to win. Quebec residents may submit any litigation respecting the conduct and awarding of a prize in this contest to the Régie des loteries et courses du Quebec.

7. Full contest rules may be obtained by sending a stamped, self-addressed envelope to: "Passport to Romance Rules Request", P.O. Box 9998, Saint John, New Brunswick, E2L 4N4.

8. Payment of taxes other than air and hotel taxes is the sole responsibility of the winner.

9. Void where prohibited by law.

RLS-DIR

PASSPORT
WIN
1 of 10 Vacations
SEE INSIDE
TO ROMANCE

VACATION SWEEPSTAKES

MONTH 1 ENTRY

Official Entry Form

Yes, enter me in the drawing for one of ten Vacations-for-Two! If I'm a winner, I'll get my choice of any of the six different destinations being offered — and I won't have to decide until after I'm notified!

Return entries with invoice in envelope provided along with Daily Travel Allowance Voucher. Each book in your shipment has two entry forms — and the more you enter, the better your chance of winning!

Name

Address   Apt.

City   State/Prov.   Zip/Postal Code

Daytime phone number _____
                              Area Code

☐ I am enclosing a Daily Travel
Allowance Voucher in the amount of $_____ Write in amount
                                        revealed beneath scratch-off

CPS-ONE